A Soldier —And a Man

by G. H. Teed

Illustrated by Val. Reading and ?

First published in the Union Jack magazine,
No. 584, New Series; 19 Dec. 1914.

Stillwoods Edition, 2022

Stillwoods.Blogspot.Ca

Catalogue Information:

Title: A Soldier—And a Man
Author: G. H. Teed (1881-1938)
Illustrated by Val. Reading and ?
First published anonymously in the Union Jack magazine, No. 584, New Series; 19 Dec. 1914.
This Edition by: Stillwoods, 2022
ISBN Canada: 978-1-989788-86-8
Blog: Stillwoods.Blogspot.Ca
Author Blog: http://ghteed.blogspot.com/
Storefront: http://www.lulu.com/spotlight/lulubook22

https://tinyurl.com/ve25d42s This link should go to a spreadsheet of all known Teed stories. The list is annotated with various information on the stories and my progress with recapturing the work. The library of Teed's stories increases almost weekly. Check at the Lulu.Com for the latest arrivals. Search for Teed…/drf

Keywords: Sexton Blake, British fictional detective, Tinker, Yvonne Cartier.

Cautionary Note: This series of books by Stillwoods are intended to make the stories of G. H. Teed, born in New Brunswick, Canada, available to collectors and researchers. The editor, or rather digitizer has not altered the original publication.

This story may contain language and racial terms that are not appropriate to today. I apologize for them; I know that the author was using his voice to excite and entertain an adventurous English audience. These works were published from 82 to 110 years ago. Most every work has characters of redeeming ethnicity within.

I hope you enjoy and share these stories; I have.
Doug Frizzle

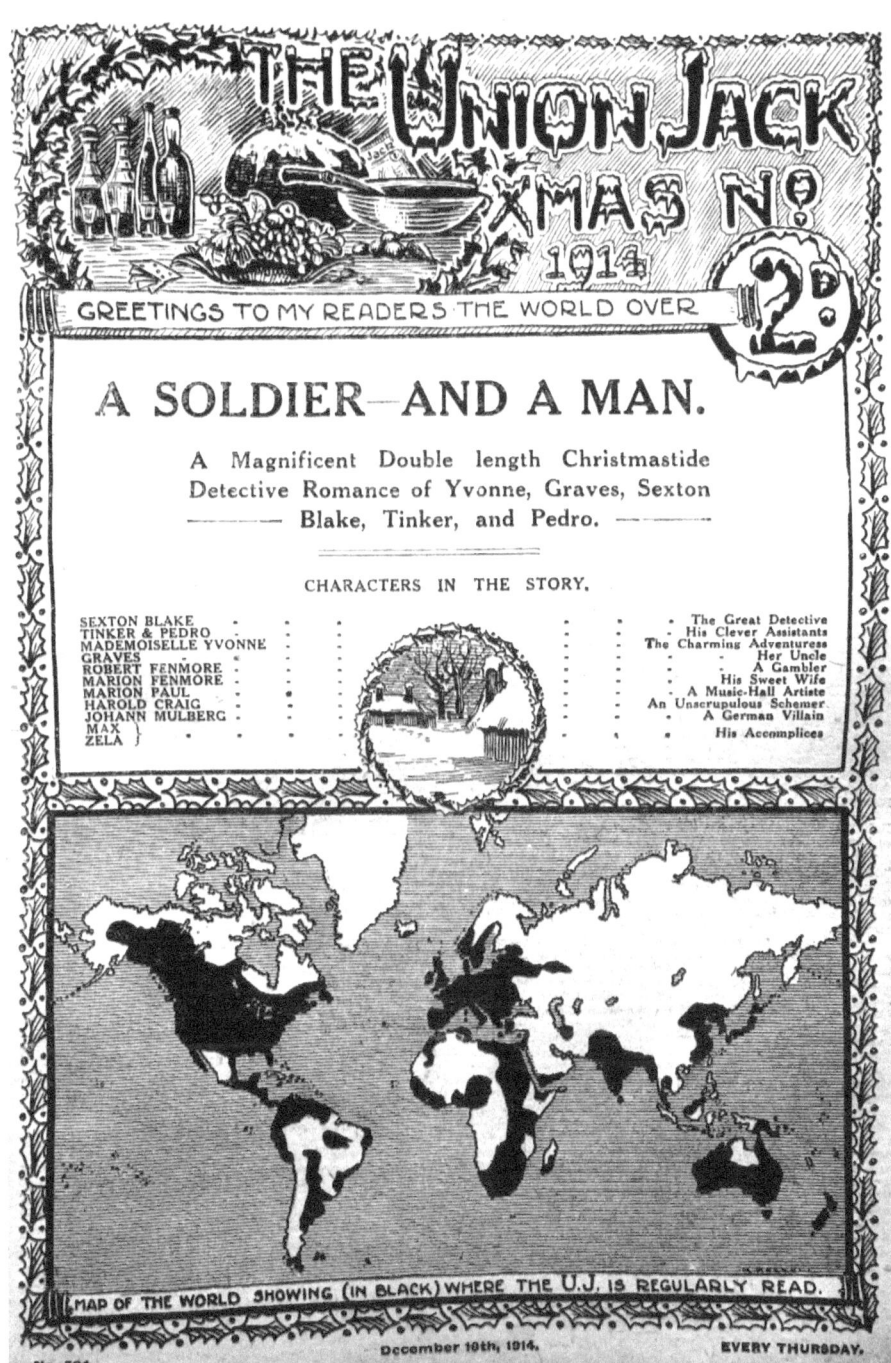

THE UNION JACK

XMAS Nº 1914

2D

GREETINGS TO MY READERS THE WORLD OVER

A SOLDIER—AND A MAN.

A Magnificent Double length Christmastide Detective Romance of Yvonne, Graves, Sexton Blake, Tinker, and Pedro.

CHARACTERS IN THE STORY.

SEXTON BLAKE	The Great Detective
TINKER & PEDRO	His Clever Assistants
MADEMOISELLE YVONNE	The Charming Adventuress
GRAVES	Her Uncle
ROBERT FENMORE	A Gambler
MARION FENMORE	His Sweet Wife
MARION PAUL	A Music-Hall Artiste
HAROLD CRAIG	An Unscrupulous Schemer
JOHANN MULBERG	A German Villain
MAX }	
ZELA }	His Accomplices

MAP OF THE WORLD SHOWING (IN BLACK) WHERE THE U.J. IS REGULARLY READ.

No. 584.   December 10th, 1914.   EVERY THURSDAY.

Greetings to my Readers the World Over.

A Magnificent Double-Length Christmas Story of Sexton Blake and Tinker.

A Magnificent Double length Christmastide Detective Romance of Yvonne, Graves, Sexton Blake, Tinker, and Pedro.

CHARACTERS IN THE STORY:

SEXTON BLAKE	The Great Detective
TINKER & PEDRO	His Clever Assistants
MADEMOISELLE YVONNE	The Charming Adventuress
GRAVES	Her Uncle
ROBERT FENMORE	A Gambler
MARION FENMORE	His Sweet Wife
MARION PAUL	A Music-Hall Artiste
HAROLD CRAIG	An Unscrupulous Schemer
JOHANN MULBERG	A German Villain
MAX \	His Accomplices
ZELA	

Introduction to this first release of 2022.

This is the first digital recovery for 2022. I have been looking at how things have come along after the disaster that Lulu.Com created in 2020, and which took me near a full year to recoup. The disaster was prompted by the withdrawal of Adobe Flash player which all of Lulu's web pages were based.

I notice that there are quite a number of Teed novels that never did make it back into the fully 'published' columns of my spreadsheet. That is to say they are not available from Barnes and Nobel and Amazon—they are strictly available from Lulu.Com.

I notice further that there is no 'Author Spotlight', a feature web page that describes my purpose in this hobby.

Supposedly one can order and search within 'My Publications' web page. This feature seems sporadic, for whatever reason.

I do notice that there are very few 'Teed' publications within Lulu.Com—so that is the best way to locate these old works. Go to Lulu.Com and search on 'Teed'.

I believe that the lowest prices are on the Lulu.Com site. Checking Amazon just now shows a significant difference in price—twice as expensive on Amazon—Canadian site!

With the release of this story, over **5 million words** by Teed are published in **162 stories**. Note that a number of stories, are available only in web page format—about 40, mostly 'Nelson Lee' novels.

There are still quite a few, over 50 stories in my archives which have yet to be digitized. I do have another life which frequently has to be serviced!

Anyhow, please enjoy! If you have questions, FrizzleDR@gmail.com will get to me.

Doug   Stillwoods

Some recent books we have been working on:

The Pirated Cargo
The Grey Domino
The Sweater's Punishment
The Great Cigarette Mystery
Black Sea Sailor –Solovyev
The Beggar in the Harem –Solovyev
The Enchanted Prince –Solovyev
The Green Portfolio
A Soldier and a Man
At the Turn of the Hour
The Sunken Schooner
The Black Emperor
The Idol's Spell
Dead Man's Rock –Q
The Adventure of the Giant Bean
Rosalie –Day
Victory Garden –Day
John Paul's Rock –Day
The Curse of the Cardews –W M Graydon
Ghosts of the Spanish Main –Dell
The House of Curtains

ROBERT FENMORE stirred and opened his eyes, gazing up at the dimly lit room uncomprehendingly. Then, as his eyes took in the familiar outlines of his valet, he yawned and sat up.

"What time is it, Bayles?" he asked thickly.

"Twelve o'clock, sir," replied the stolid-looking valet. "Shall I prepare your bath, sir?"

"Shortly," snapped Fenmore. "Twelve o'clock, eh? What time did I get in, Bayles?"

"A little before seven, sir."

"Gad! I did have a stiff night. Where is Mrs. Fenmore?"

"She went out about ten o'clock, sir. Shall I draw the blinds, sir? It is a very fine day."

"Ugh! Not yet, Bayles. I couldn't stand sunlight now. So Mrs. Fenmore went out, eh? Alone?"

"No, sir. Mr. Craig accompanied her."

"H'm!" grunted Fenmore to himself. "My esteemed cousin Harold seems to be always accompanying her lately." Then aloud he said:

"Did she leave any word for me, Bayles?"

"No, sir."

Fenmore grunted again, then said irritably:

"For heaven's sake get me a drink, and don't stand there looking at me like an owl. I suppose, in your heart, you think I am all kinds of terrible things, eh? I expect in the servants' hall you hold forth amongst you upon my iniquities."

"I am not paid to think, sir, and I never discuss my master with others," returned the valet a little stiffly. "Here is your drink, sir. And now shall I prepare the bath?"

"Yes—yes," snapped Fenmore. "Do anything as long as you get out of my sight."

As the valet moved towards a door at the far end of the room, Bob Fenmore tossed off the drink of whisky at a single gulp, and leaning back in bed, stared moodily at the ceiling.

"Hang the luck!" he muttered after a few minutes. "Another three thousand last night. Will I never win? If I punt I lose, and if I take the bank I lose. My luck is dead out. Well, it can't keep up always; but by jingo, if it doesn't change soon I will be stony. Hang the warnings! They make me loathe myself, and yet I know that to-night, and tomorrow night, and every night after I will play again, until I win back what I have lost. Gad! to think of the money I have gone through in the past six months.

"Marion had a hundred thousand when we were married, six months ago, and now it is all gone but thirty thousand. I hope to goodness she doesn't find out what a hole I have made in it. And the worst of it is I must have more. Well, by heavens, the luck must turn soon, and then I will repay her what her I have taken."

He was interrupted by the entrance of Bayles, who announced that the bath was ready, and with a grunt of acknowledgment Fenmore sprang out of bed. The room itself was a most luxurious apartment, furnished richly but quietly, and containing all the choicest appurtenances which a gentleman of taste and the means to gratify it gathers about him. Had Bayles been permitted to draw the curtains, it could have been seen that the windows looked out on to a quiet square in one of the most exclusive neighbourhoods of London, and that the house itself was what is known as "a gentleman's desirable residence."

Robert Fenmore himself—or Bob as he was known about town— was a tall, well-built, muscular man of about thirty. A year ago there had been no better looking, cleaner living man in London than he; but one night he had accompanied some companions to a private gambling den, and had been seized by the fever in its worst form. From that moment he had been a changed man.

He had forsaken all his old haunts, had given up his polo, had adopted the unhealthy hours made necessary by his new life, and worse than all, had begun to drink too much. He had felt the gambler's need for stimulant, and had yielded to it. Only those with whom he gambled knew exactly how heavily he was losing; but it was common talk that he was going a stiff pace, and when six months before he had married a wealthy orphan, people had shaken their heads.

Some said he had married her for her money, and that he would soon run through it, as he was going through his own. Others hinted that he had married her simply to cut in ahead of his cousin Harold Craig, with whom he had never been very cordial. Still others, more charitable, said that Marion Straight was so sweet and charming in herself that any man would be lucky to gain her as wife. Bob Fenmore had paused once about five months before, to ask himself why he had married, and had flushed with shame when the better side of his nature had told him that Marion's money had been a big incentive to him. He had given up gambling for a week, and had made a strong effort to play the part of the home-loving husband; but at the end of that time the fever had conquered him, and he had gone back to the tables more fiercely than ever.

So he and Marion had drifted farther and farther apart, until now, they scarcely even saw each other from one day's end to another.

To the world Marion Fenmore presented a smiling face. She had too much pride in her nature to permit outsiders to see the scars on her heart, and only she herself knew about the long nights of agony when she lay in bed dry-eyed and sleepless, staring up into the darkness, and suffering, as only a woman can suffer, who has given her whole being to a man. She was only twenty-one, and too young and inexperienced to grapple with the terrible octopus which was steadily overcoming her husband.

Yet her love for him had never faltered. He had come into her life when his cousin Harold Craig had been paying her some attention, and Fenmore's sunny ways and frank, charming manner had swept her off her feet. She had heard rumours of his gambling it is true, but like many a woman before, she had prayed a prayer and felt that the very strength of the love she bore him would oust all other desires from his life.

Disillusionment had come all too quickly. Scarcely had they returned from the honeymoon when Fenmore had started gambling again. Marion had said nothing, but had brought to bear all her love to endeavour to conquer the thing which was threatening her happiness.

But the day had come when she had been compelled to acknowledge defeat, and from that time on, husband and wife had been as strangers in the same house. None could tell just when Harold Craig had begun to come frequently to the house. His visits had started shortly after Fenmore had returned to his old ways, and they had grown more numerous in an unintrusive way, until now he was looked upon as one of the household.

He had accompanied Marion on her rides and walks only occasionally at first, but lately this had become practically a daily occurrence, and she, heart-sick and blind to all else through her yearning for her husband, never guessed the black purpose in Craig's heart. Nor did she see the sly looks and nods which had begun to appear on people's faces when she and Craig were seen together.

And this was the condition of affairs in the household of Bob Fenmore on the morning this story opens.

Fenmore paused before a long mirror, and gazed at his own reflection before passing on to his bath. He was not so far lost to all sense of shame that he couldn't read the disgust he saw on the face in the mirror, at the puffy cheeks and blood-shot eyes which both told their own tale.

Then he shrugged and swung on his heel, walking unsteadily towards the door of the bathroom. Half an hour later he reappeared bathed, shaved, and wearing an elaborate dressing-gown. He certainly looked fresher than when he entered the bath, but when he struck a match to light a cigarette, his hand shook nervously, revealing the havoc which had been wrought. While he had been bathing, Bayles had laid out breakfast on a small table, and now he drew aside the curtains, letting the warm sunlight flood the room.

Fenmore frowned, but said nothing, and while he nibbled half-heartedly at the tasty food, glanced over his letters. The manner in which he tossed most of them aside, seemed to indicate that they held no interest for him; but down near the bottom of the pile, he came upon one which he seized eagerly.

Breaking the seal he drew out a single folded sheet of paper, and spread it out. As he read the contents, a flush came into his cheeks, and his eyes gleamed with pleasure. It was thus that he looked when the fever of gambling enthralled him, and now it was gripping him again, for in the letter was news which was good—to the gambler. It read as follows:

"Dear Sir,—We have examined the securities which you left with us at our last interview, and beg to say that we shall be pleased to make you a sixty per cent. advance upon them. Should you call in the course of the day, we can arrange to hand you our cheque for the amount. The rate of interest will be the same as before.

"We are, dear sir, etc.,

"Borrow, Wills & Field."

Fenmore stuffed the letter in his pocket, and made a rapid mental calculation.

"Sixty per cent, and the securities I left totalled eight thousand. That means four thousand eight hundred. I lost three thousand last night, and on that gave I.O.U.'s for sixteen hundred. When I pay those out of the four thousand eight hundred I shall get from the solicitors, it will leave me three thousand odd to go on with. And, if my luck only changes and gives me a decent run, I shall make that three thousand odd win me back all I have lost and more.

"Capital! And by the way, I mustn't forget to make a memorandum of those securities. That reduces Marion's stuff to twenty-two thousand. Gad! I have made a hole in it. But never mind. I'll soon pay it back with interest.

"Now I must dress and go round to the solicitors at once. I shall just have about time to fix matters up and get the cheque turned into cash before the bank closes."

He rose as he came to this decision, and as he walked across to the door of his dressing-room, a faint smile of pleasurable anticipation tinged the corners of his lips.

Bob Fenmore was once more walking arm-in-arm with the god of gambling, and while that fiend held sway he thought not of his home, his wife, or—his cousin, Harold Craig.

He dressed more rapidly than usual, and when he emerged from the dressing-room, found Bayles standing ready with his hat and stick.

"Has Mrs. Fenmore returned yet, Bayles?" asked Fenmore carelessly, as he lighted a cigarette and picked up his gloves.

"No, sir. Any message for her, sir?"

"You can say that I shall dine at the club, and will not be home till late."

"Very good, sir."

Fenmore took his hat and stick and made for the door.

He paused with his fingers on the handle.

"You needn't wait up to-night, Bayles. I shall be late—as usual."

With that he opened the door and passed out. When Bayles was sure he had really gone, he made swiftly for the window; and standing close to the curtains stood peering forth. He heard a whistle down below, saw a taxi leave the rank and draw up in front of the house, then the door slammed, and the taxi drove off.

"Still at it," muttered the valet with a sigh. "Heaven only knows where it will all end. Every night of his life, and from what I know of him, he ain't no light punter. He must be dropping thousands. And while he is off gambling, his cousin is hanging round the house at all hours. It's rough on the mistress, and she's too much cut up over the master's going on, to see that snake's purpose. Curse him, I hate him!"

With that brief but vigorous expression about Harold Craig, Bayles turned back from the window and went ahead with his duties.

As for Bob Fenmore, he was already speeding Citywards, towards the offices of Barrow, Wills & Field, the solicitors who had in hand the business of raising a loan on certain of Mrs. Fenmore's securities which Fenmore had in his charge. These were located in a musty building not far from Grays Inn, and on arriving there, Fenmore was shown at once into the office of Mr. Barrow, the senior partner.

"Ah, Mr. Fenmore," he said, rising, "you are prompt. You received our letter."

Fenmore shook hands and sat down in the chair which the solicitor indicated.

"Yes, thanks. It came this morning. I am glad you were able to arrange the loan on the securities. Between ourselves, I need the money rather urgently."

"Oh, it was not hard to fix it up on securities of that description. In fact, we could have got seventy-five per cent, without trouble; but as you yourself had said sixty, we did not make the loan more."

"Quite right—quite right. Sixty per cent. will be ample for my purpose. Er—"

"'You would like a cheque for the amount?" suggested the solicitor, correctly reading his client's hesitating expression.

"Thanks, I should. And—er—I was wondering if you could manage to let me have the amount in notes. It would be an—er—convenience."

"Why, certainly, Mr. Fenmore. If you will wait here I can send round to the bank and get the sum. How would you like it?"

"Oh, in—er—fifties and tens—yes, that will do. About four thousand in fifties and the odd eight hundred in tens."

The solicitor made a note of the particulars and pressed a button. To the clerk who answered his summons he said:

"Send Jameson here."

The clerk disappeared, and a few moments later an old man appeared.

"Jameson," said the solicitor, "I want you to take this cheque to the bank and get the sum in cash. Get four thousand in fifty-pound notes and eight hundred in ten-pound notes."

The old man, evidently the chief clerk, took the cheque and

bowed himself out.

For twenty minutes or so the solicitor and his client talked trivialities until Jameson returned and handed his employer the money. Then they fixed up the few formalities necessary, and Bob Fenmore pocketed the notes with a sigh of relief. They felt very comfortable in his pocket, and with his ammunition replenished, he felt able to break the worst run of luck in the world. Such is the perpetual optimism of the gambler. Bidding the solicitor good-bye, he made his way out and hailed a taxi.

From Gray's Inn he drove straight to his club, and took the letters which the hall-porter handed him. With these in his hand he entered the smoking-room and chose a comfortable armchair, well removed from the window. Then he ordered a drink, and while waiting for it to be brought, glanced at his letters. As had been the case with those which he had received at his house, only one seemed to interest him, and this one he tore open quickly. A faint elusive scent arose as he did so, and though the contents of the letter were brief, they evidently gave him pleasure, for he smiled as he read:

"We played too late last night, and to-day I have a headache. But never mind, cherie, take me to dinner tonight. I feel that you will cheer me up, and perhaps we shall play again later. You poor boy, you did have beastly luck last night; but to-night I feel that luck is with us.   "M."

And had Bob Fenmore cared to tell one what "M" meant, he would have said only what all his world knew—that it referred to Marion Paul, the well-known music-hall star who had taken all London by storm. And that was, so the world said, another of Bob Fenmore's iniquities.

That he should gamble as he did was bad enough, but that he should flout convention by dining night after night with a music-hall artiste, no matter how popular she might be, was another matter. And the same world was spending much of its time in watching the course of events.

Now, as a matter of fact, Bob Fenmore did dine often with Marion Paul, and found a certain pleasure in her society. To him she acted the same as alcohol or gaming—she stimulated him and the thoughts of her made him forget the ugly spectres which sometimes rose before him. But he had no other regard for her; though she accompanied him night after night to the tables, he never gave her a thought from the moment he entered the gaming-room.

But the world didn't know this, and even if it had, it would have shrugged disbelievingly. That is only the way of the world. Yet there were a few things about his relationship with Marion Paul of which even Bob Fenmore himself was unaware. One was that his introduction to her had been a carefully-planned affair. Another was that in case he showed signs of flagging in his devotion to gaming, that Marion Paul was pledged to fan the flame and keep it burning brightly.

And the third was that she was to use all her arts to lure him on until when his finish came it would be utterly complete.

For the relationship of Marion Paul with Bob Fenmore—a relationship of which we shall hear more as this record of events proceeds, was but one of the carefully-planned little moves which had been fathered by Fenmore's cousin, Harold Craig. But Fenmore never dreamed of such a thing, and took the homage which Marion Paul seemed to give him as a tribute to his own attractions.

Bob Fenmore was due for an awakening one day, and when it came it was bound to be a severe one. He was playing the game particularly stiff, and when a man does that he must pay a proportionate price. But as yet he was only conscious that he must follow the beckoning finger of chance; and so when he had read Marion Paul's note, he sat down at a desk and scrawled off a hurried reply, telling her that he would be charmed to have her dine with him, and that he would call for her early.

He posted this at once, and then strolled to the card-room, where he soon became engaged in a mild rubber of bridge, and where he would so remain until it were time to call for Marion Paul.

Now, so absorbed was Bob Fenmore in his own affairs that he had taken no notice of what others were in the club smoking-room when he entered. Had he done so, he might have seen that more than one pair of eyes were cast in his direction, and that the owners turned to one another with significant looks on their faces.

But he had seen nothing of this, and consequently did not know that while he sat whetting his appetite for the big game of the evening to come by playing bridge, he was being discussed back in the smoking-room by three men, who sat together in a corner.

"He must be mad," one of them was saying. "He is the talk of the town, and it is a wonder to me the club committee haven't done something about it before this."

The speaker, Lord Maldon, frowned at the ceiling as he made the observation, for he was one of the oldest members of the Ocean Club, and it angered him to see one of the members making himself conspicuous as Fenmore was doing.

The next speaker was the man who sat facing Lord Maldon, and who looked indolently handsome with his well-cut suit of grey setting off the silver white of his pointed beard and well-trimmed moustache. Graves, a popular member of the club, and uncle of Mademoiselle Yvonne, who by her daring exploits some time before had set three continents buzzing.

"Oh, I don't know, Maldon!" he said lazily. "We must be lenient with the young. I grant you Fenmore is going it pretty stiff; but I feel confident he will shake down all right. I believe he is sound at heart, and that should eventually be his Salvation."

Then the third member of the party spoke up. He was a small man who wore mutton-chop whiskers, and when speaking always peered over the top of his glasses, which were continually perched down below the bridge of his nose and invariably falling off. Yet he was one of the shrewdest company lawyers in the City, and Anthony Carew could command practically whatever fee he named.

"I could have some patience with Fenmore if it was only the gambling. I knew his father well, and a finer, straighter man never lived. He, too, had the gaming fever in his younger days, but got over it safely. When he married he gave it up entirely, and from that time on was a model citizen. But the boy—I am afraid of what the result may be with him. He seems to lack something which his father possessed.

"He has married one of the most charming girls in the world, yet look at him now. Only six months has passed, and already he is the talk of the town. It is this association of his name with that of Marion Paul which makes me fear what the end may be. I am afraid you are too lenient, Graves. Maldon may be a little too severe in his judgment, but it is a very bad condition of affairs."

"Not only that, but he has left his wife alone almost from the day they were married, and people are beginning to talk," put in Lord Maldon bluntly.

"You mean about the frequency with which Craig is seen with her?" asked Graves.

"Yes."

"Well, I don't know anything about it," went on Graves, lighting a fresh cigarette; "but I acknowledge his treatment of his wife—than whom a sweeter, more charming lady never lived—and his public attention to Marion Paul, are bad elements but still I think he will come out right. It might be a good thing if he were brought up with a round turn and shown what an imbecile he is making of himself."

"One wouldn't get thanked for one's pains," remarked Lord Maldon. "Are you taking a hand in a rubber, Graves?"

The latter tossed away his cigarette and shook his head.

"No; not this afternoon. I may this evening, but I must toddle along home now. I have an appointment with my niece, and she is not a young lady whom it is wise to keep waiting too long."

His two cronies smiled at the remark, and grunted an adieu as he strolled away, then they continued their conversation.

Graves sent a boy for his hat and stick, and passing out of the club hailed a taxi. Entering, he ordered the man to drive to Queen Anne's Gate, and on his arrival there opened the door of Yvonne's flat with his latchkey and walked straight through to the room at the end of the hall where she sat at the desk busily writing. Knowing he would receive no attention until she finished, he tossed his hat and stick aside and reached for a cigarette. As she sat a long spear of sunlight fell on Yvonne's burnished hair, and lit it up like a mass of fine dull gold.

It fell in a bewildering mass about her neck, and Graves frankly admired it as he smoked. If there was one thing on earth more precious to him than the dead and gone sister in Australia, it was that sister's child, Yvonne, the girl who sat before him, and upon whom he lavished all the love of father and mother and brother.

Yet it was an accepted fact between them that it was the brain beneath those same burnished coils which guided and ruled their lives, and always one of the languid ones. Graves was well content that this should be so. He had consumed half of his cigarette before Yvonne laid down her pen and turned.

"Well," she smiled, "you did remember that we were to have tea together this afternoon, did you? I suppose you could not tear yourself away from your cronies until the last moment."

Graves grinned a trifle sheepishly.

"There was to be a game of bridge," he said, "but I refrained."

Yvonne rose, and as she passed him on her way to ring the bell, patted his shoulder fondly.

"Never mind, you can make up for it this evening. I wanted you to come home this afternoon particularly, as I have something to discuss with you."

"What's in the wind?" asked Graves, with a look of mock alarm on his face.

"Nothing which will drag you from your favourite chair at the club," laughed Yvonne. Then, to the servant who had entered: "Serve tea here, Alec.

"No," she continued, when the man had gone, "I only want to discuss the present political outlook with you. I have been going over the situation to-day, and to me it looks bad. What is the talk amongst the clubs?"

"It is difficult to get a definite opinion," answered Graves. "Of course, the fact that we have had so many European crises in the last ten years caused a certain impression to prevail that we shall fix up the present difficulty in the same way. But, of course, Germany's refusal to discuss the Austro-Servian trouble with Britain, France, and Russia is causing a good deal of uneasiness."

Yvonne nodded thoughtfully, and waited until Alec had arranged the tea-things. Then, when he had again withdrawn, she said:

"There is, of course, a lot in that. But to me there seems to be a something in this present crisis which has not been in any of the others. I have been going over the share situation for the past two years, and do you know that, with very few exceptions, the whole list has been dropping steadily!

"There have been no violent drops which would cause comment, but a steady decline which has continued from that period of time. Now, shares are, in a way, the pulse of the international situation. When they have gone as they have during the past two years there is something radically wrong. There have been rallies, of course, but they have never held, and the market can only be described as sick. Look at the Bourses of the world during the past few days. They are one and all on the way to becoming demoralised. And that means that the big financial sources which control the situation are nervous, and are retrenching as rapidly as possible. There will be no money for shares if the Governments of Europe need untold millions for war."

"I heard to-day that the London Stock Exchange was going to

close," said Graves.

"And I have but this afternoon received a cipher message from one of my agents in Paris, saying that the Paris Bourse was demoralised, and that it would close to-night. I tell you, uncle, I believe we are on the verge of the great war so long predicted, and if it comes, no man may read the ending. So convinced do I feel that serious trouble is brewing, that I have made a memorandum of all my speculative shares, and tonight I shall cable a selling order to New York to dispose of the whole list.

"If the Stock Exchanges of the world do close, New York is bound to be the last available market, and before it is forced to close, half Europe will be throwing over their holdings, and panic prices will rule even there."

"I believe you are dead right, Yvonne," remarked Graves admiringly. "I wish I had your head for finance."

"One such in the family is enough," smiled Yvonne. Then she grew serious again. "There is something else I want to talk to you about, uncle. What is the trouble between Bob and Marion Fenmore? I saw her in Bond Street to-day with a man, and although her lips smiled, she had tragedy in her eyes. Have you heard anything? Marion is one of my dearest friends, and if she is in trouble I should do anything I could to help her."

Graves set down his teacup, and looked embarrassed.

"Why—er—why—er—I believe—"

"Now, see here, uncle," broke in Yvonne, "when you begin to answer one of my questions with your 'why—er's,' I always know you are keeping things back. Come along, 'fess up! You have heard something, and I mean to know what it is."

Graves laughed outright.

"Well, as a matter of fact, you caught me off my guard," he said. "And it is a bit of a coincidence, too, for we were discussing that very thing just before I left the club."

"What is the matter? What is being said? Has Bob Fenmore started gambling again?"

"I believe he is playing a little," returned Graves cautiously. "To tell the truth, the talk is pretty bad, and—"

"Well, tell me the rest," prompted Yvonne, when he hesitated. "You know I shall make you tell me everything before I finish, so you may as well yield gracefully."

"It is said that he must be losing a good deal of money, and that, of course, it must be his wife's, because he had gone through every penny of his own before he married. She was well off, but no fortune can stand the treatment he is giving hers. It seems, too, that he is making a bit of a fool of himself over Marion Paul, of the Sphinx Theatre; and now gossip is busy with the name of his cousin, Harold Craig.

"I presume that was the man you saw with Marion Fenmore this afternoon. He seems to spend most of his time in her neighbourhood since Bob started gambling again. That is all I know, and I wish you hadn't asked me about it. Now reward me by giving me another cup of tea."

Yvonne poured out the tea mechanically. Her face was very grave, and a frown rested on her fair brow. She had been sharp enough to see that Marion Fenmore was not as happy as she would have the world believe, but she had not dreamed that things were as bad as they were. She knew her uncle thoroughly—she knew how kindly, how lenient, was his nature, and if he said as much as he had about Bob Fenmore, she was quite aware that the actual facts must be far worse.

She was honestly worried, for Marion Straight had been a very dear friend of hers, and Yvonne knew how she had loved Bob Fenmore when she married him. Yvonne had known—as all the world knew—about the gambling he had done previous to his marriage, and, like a good many others, she had hoped that Marion's love would succeed in making him forget the lure of the tables.

Now that she had some inkling of the truth, her blood boiled with rage against the man who could take anything so fine as Marion Straight and break her upon the torture wheel of neglect. Her eyes were gleaming angrily when she spoke again.

"How dare he!" she said fiercely. "How dare he do such a thing! Is he blind that he cannot see what Marion is suffering? Wasn't it enough that he lost all his own money, without frittering away every penny of hers? It is contemptible! And as if that weren't sufficient, he must needs have his name bandied about with that of a music-hall artiste. Marion Paul may be all right for anything I know, but he is a married man— married scarcely six months, and Marion Paul knows it!

And what does he mean by permitting gossip to connect his

cousin's name with that of his wife? I never met Harold Craig, but if the man I saw with Marion Fenmore in Bond Street to-day is he, I must say I don't like him. His eye is not good and the eyes are the windows of the soul."

"Fenmore certainly ought to catch hold of himself," remarked Graves. "He must have lost an awful lot of Marion's money."

"And will go on and on and on until he loses it all," said Yvonne. "Then what will the future be? How long has this been going on, uncle?"

"Why, I believe he began again shortly after the honeymoon."

Yvonne's white teeth came together with a click.

"Do you know where he plays?"

"Frileti's, I believe—you know, the big private gaming place off Wilton Crescent."

Yvonne nodded.

"If he is playing there he is playing for big stakes. They have no use for small fry at Frileti's. But I thought the place had been sold or closed up, or something."

"It was closed for a time after the police raid a few months back, but it has been opened by other people since, and is being run as a select place for a few safe people. It takes trouble to get introduced there, but once you are in you can have the run of the place, I am told. From what I hear, the play is very high indeed."

Yvonne rose and paced up and down the room for a few minutes in silence. Then she paused before Graves.

"Uncle," she said, "this thing has upset me a lot. I don't want to judge Bob Fenmore on pure gossip, but if he is treating Marion as it seems he must be, and if he is going through her money as he went through his own, something must be done.

"She is too good and sweet to be made the victim of his madness, and if she can't combat the trouble herself, I shall do so for her. I want you to arrange for me to go to Frileti's to-night. If he is playing, I shall watch him, and then I shall know myself exactly how matters stand."

"It is a dangerous business mixing up between man and wife," warned Graves. "But I don't see what harm it can do to get at the truth of some of these stories about Fenmore. It might be a good idea to go to Frileti's and watch him play. Do you want me to go with you?"

"No, thanks; I think I prefer to go alone. You can arrange it, can't you?"

"Nothing easier. Lord Maldon will fix it up in no time. I'll get him to write a note when I go to the club this evening, and you can call for it on your way. Only do be careful, Yvonne. Fenmore may come out all right if left alone."

Yvonne shook her head angrily.

"If I am mistaken, I shall be the first to admit it; but if he is doing the things attributed to him, then let him look out, I shall never forget the expression which I saw in Marion Fenmore's eyes to-day. She looked like a little fawn which had been beaten down by the hand which had always stroked her, and was so stupefied with the shock that she saw nothing else about her.

"And the man—Harold Craig—he was like the wolf lying in wait to rush upon her. Oh, I may be wrong, but I am going to get to the bottom of this affair."

With that she abruptly left the room, and as she disappeared, Graves sighed.

"If she says she will, she certainly will," he murmured. Then he lighted a fresh cigarette and picked up a paper.

Yvonne saw eight or ten punters at the table, and approaching watched the play for a little, examining the players as she did so. But at last she had to confess that in none of the rooms she had visited were there any signs of either Bob Fenmore or Marion Paul.

II.

FRILETI'S was crowded. From the street outside the casual wayfarer would never have suspected that the large, dignified house which bore the number 42 upon its door, and was in darkness from top to bottom, was one of the most luxuriously furnished gambling dens in London, and that nightly its great rooms were crowded by the elite of the gambling world. Yet such was the case, and on this particular night it seemed more packed than ever.

Little recked the habitues of the place if the dire mutterings of war could be heard from one end of Europe to the other. Cared not they if emperors went mad and dynasties rocked to their foundations. What were these issues beside the great and all-absorbing one as to which pocket the little ball in the roulette wheel would choose for a resting-place, or which colour or combination would be uppermost in rouge et noir? Those problems were far more absorbing, and the fact that the tables continually showed a strong disinclination to go as the players thought they should go but served to whet the appetite.

Some day—the gambler's some day—they must change. And not only because play was high at Frileti's was the place popular. It had a rule which appealed to those who wished to game and yet desired to conceal their identity, and that was that all ladies and what gentlemen wished were to come masked. In this way many a dame of the haute monde rubbed shoulders with the lady of the music-hall chorus, and knew it not.

Many a peer brushed sleeves with his more prosperous bookmaker, and, guessed not. And it is a fact that on more than one occasion a prosperous butler, grown opulent from a systematic robbing of his master, had played elbow to elbow with that same master. There were all sorts and conditions in Frileti's, but to gain entrance two things were essential.

You must be introduced by an unquestionable source, and you must have money. As Graves had truly said, it was no place for the timid, and strict secrecy was necessary, for the simple reason that Scotland Yard, though quiescent for the time being, might swoop down at any moment, as it had swooped down when Frileti himself had run the place.

No one knew exactly who did run it now, and few cared. It was sufficient for the customers to know that it was a safe place to indulge the passion which ruled them, and they asked no more. Had they known who really was behind the place, there would have been astonishment in more than one quarter.

On the ground floor both of the large front rooms were given over to refreshments. In the one to the right anything that one wished from beer to champagne could be obtained, and nothing was charged. In the room to the left there was always a well-stocked buffet, and it was sufficient to be within the house, whether playing or not, to pick and choose as much and as often as one wished.

There was certainly a genius of a sort behind the new Frileti's. Upstairs on the first floor were the gaming rooms, and here, too, one could demand liquid refreshment when one so desired. The large room to the right was given over to roulette and rouge et noir. In the room to the rear of that a game of chemin de fer was always in progress, and again to the rear of that was the poker room.

The front room on the left was given over to another, though slightly more moderate, game of chemin de fer, and the room to the rear of it was the faro room. There was another room beyond that again, and of all the gaming rooms this alone had the door closed. That a game of some sort must be in progress there all knew, but only the regulars were aware that it contained a faro table where only the stiffest stakes were laid.

A few—very few of the most reckless were admitted to this room, and it was said that the masked dealer at that table was the mysterious proprietor of the house himself.

To this abode of the god of chance came Yvonne that night. She had spent some considerable time over her personal appearance before leaving Queen Anne's Gate, and it would have taken a penetrating eye indeed to pierce the disguise which hid her identity, though it was simple withal.

The greatest change was in the hair of burnished bronze, like which there was none other in all London. This had been ruthlessly changed to ebony black, and when her eyes of soft morning blue, and her little straight nose had been concealed by a black silken mask, all the world could see were a pair of delicately curved red lips, a white firm chin, and a throat of alabaster, faultless in its perfection, and disappearing with gracious curves beneath the rich evening gown of sea green.

The note which Lord Maldon had written at Graves' request had secured her entree without demur, and guided by a gorgeously uniformed attendant, she had at once ascended to the floor above, where a maid had taken her wraps.

The evening was in full progress, for Yvonne had not come early, and choosing to wander about before settling down to the definite quest which had brought her, she strolled into the large room on the right, where the roulette and rouge et noir games were in full swing.

Pushing her way through the crowd which thronged the roulette table, she stood behind a chair occupied by a stout man who had taken the precaution to mask himself. He seemed to be having a fairly good run of it, and when observation had shown Yvonne what the stakes were, she opened the gold purse which she had brought, and tossed a couple of gold pieces on the same number which was being backed by the man seated in front of her.

The number came up, and Yvonne gathered up the heap of gold which the croupier imperturbably pushed towards her with his little rake. And with just as much lack of expression did he rake in or pay out the other stakes on the table. Yvonne backed her luck for another turn, playing on the same number, and when it came up once again many envious glances were shot at the slim, beautifully gowned girl who gathered up her winnings so nonchalantly.

Then Yvonne let the turn go by, and drawing back a little began to scan the faces of those about her. Surreptitiously she made a close examination of each one. She had no idea whether Bob Fenmore would be masked or not, but she felt that even if he were, her experienced eyes could pierce such a disguise as that. When she had finished her scrutiny, however, she was certain that Fenmore was not in that room.

So she backed away from the table and strolled through to the room where a game of chemin de fer was in progress. There were scarcely half a dozen playing here, and four were women. The other two were both elderly men, unmasked, and having the undeniable stamp of the bookmaker about them.

Yvonne scarcely paused here, but kept on to the poker room. Two tables were going, seven players, all men, at each; and here, too, there were no masks. She swept them with a rapid gaze, and decided that if Bob Fenmore was in the place she must look elsewhere, for he was in none of the three rooms which she had examined. So she made her way back past the chemin de fer players, through the roulette and rouge et noir room, and crossed the hall to the front room on the left where the more general game of chemin was in swing.

There were over a score of people in this apartment, and with scarcely a single exception they were masked. From their clothes and bearing, Yvonne knew them to be the better class of the habitues, and began to feel that if Bob Fenmore were there she might find him amongst these.

Under pretence of watching the play, she closely scanned the assembled players one by one. She was not looking for Fenmore to be alone, for instinct told her that if what was said about him and Marion Paul was true, the music-hall star would probably be with him. Consequently, she paid as much attention to the women as to the men. But search as she would she could not fix upon a single person who might have been either Fenmore or Marion Paul. She turned away with a little twinge of disappointment, and from an attendant took a small glass of wine which she sipped slowly.

Thru she moved along to the room adjoining where the faro game was on. She saw eight or ten punters at the table, and approaching watched the play for a little, examining the players as she did so. But at last she had to confess that in none of the rooms she had visited were there any signs of either Bob Fenmore or Marion Paul.

Perhaps he was not playing to-night, or, if so, it was just possible that he had not arrived yet. She decided to wait for a time, at least, so pressing forward at the faro table, where the full thirteen cards of a suit were represented in ivory and ebony embedded in the table, she placed a bet on the six to win and the ace to lose, following simply the dictates of chance, and no particular system. Other bets were laid here and there, either for a win or lose or both, according as the player fancied, then the dealer drew the cards from the little silver dealing box, announcing as he did so "the five wins and the nine loses."

Since neither of Yvonne's bets were affected by this call, she left them as they were, and waited while the dealer gathered in or paid out all wagers on these two numbers according to the way they had gone. Then came the curt:

"Make your bets, please," and again the monotonous call of the cards. This time it was "the six wins and the king loses."

Yvonne's, bet on the six was thus affected, and since she had backed it to win she collected instead of losing. Stuffing her winnings in her purse, she waited while the usual formalities were gone through, then came the call of the dealer again: "The ace wins and the seven loses."

Yvonne had backed the ace to lose, and since it had won she therefore lost her stake. But that worried her little. She was already well ahead on the roulette, and her win on the six at faro had just offset her loss on the ace, so she was square at that table.

She turned away with a little shrug, intending to go back to the chemin room, when suddenly she drew back sharply and stood gazing at a man and woman who had just entered the faro room. The man was unmasked, and over the shoulders of the people between she saw that it was no other than Bob Fenmore. The woman wore a black silken mask, as did Yvonne, but it proved no effective disguise to her, for beneath it Yvonne had not the slightest difficulty in recognising the identity of Marion Paul, the music-hall star.

At first Yvonne thought they were coming to the faro table, but in a moment she saw that was not the case. They kept on past it, and went straight to the door at the other end of the room.

Fenmore did not pause to knock, but turned the handle at once and stood aside for his companion to enter. Then he followed, and the door closed after him. Beneath her mask Yvonne frowned in puzzlement. What was the room which they had entered? There could be no question but that it was a gaming apartment of some description.

Then suddenly the truth flashed upon her, and she berated herself for not having thought of it before. She knew quite enough of such resorts to be aware that they all had a room somewhere which was given over to the few who played for very large stakes, and since Bob Fenmore had gone into that room, it was her purpose to follow.

Hastily she drew aside and opened her purse, running through the money she had with her. She found something like sixty pounds in gold, three hundred odd in fives and tens, and then from a secret place in the bag she drew two banknotes for five hundred each—a reserve fund without which Yvonne never travelled.

That made almost fourteen hundred pounds—quite sufficient for a first night's play at even the biggest game. Crumpling all the notes together, she closed her bag and strolled towards the chemin room, and sought out an attendant.

"The play in these rooms is not high enough for me," she said carelessly. "Is there no other room where the stakes are larger?"

The man hesitated for a moment, then replied:

"There is another room, madam, where faro is played for high stakes, but I do not know if the places are all made up. I will inquire if you wish."

"Do so, please. I shall wait here."

The man hurried away, and Yvonne watched him pass through the adjoining room and knock at the door behind which Bob Fenmore and his companion had disappeared. Evidently he received a summons to enter, for after a moment's wait he turned the handle and passed inside, closing the door after him. Two or three minutes passed before he reappeared, and when he did so he came straight towards Yvonne.

"I have inquired if you may play there, madam, and it will be quite all right if you wish to do so."

"Thank you. Am I to pass straight through?"

"Yes, please, madam."

Yvonne turned and walked back through the faro room until she reached the closed door. She gave a little preliminary knock on it, but without waiting for any summons turned the handle and entered. Immediately she got inside she closed the door after her, and stood for a moment surveying her surroundings.

The room was much smaller than the others, but even more richly furnished than any. The walls were hung with heavy figured tapestry, while scattered here and there were several soft divans loaded with cushions. On a buffet at one side were drinks and several kinds of sandwiches, and on another table a profusion of cigars and cigarettes. In the very centre of the room was the faro table, round which only five players were gathered, and Yvonne saw with a little thrill that Bob Fenmore and Marion Paul were amongst the five.

At one end of the table sat the case-keeper—the case-keeper at faro keeps tracks of all the cards which have been called by the dealer, so that when the call is reduced to the last two in the dealer's box, the punter knows which two those cards are, but, of course, has no idea which will win and which will lose, or in other words, which will come out first and which second— while facing the players sat the dealer. The case-keeper, Yvonne saw in a single glance, was simply a professional, but the dealer had something of mystery about him, for, like many of his clients, his face was well covered by a large black mask, from beneath which his voice came low and muffled.

Beside Bob Fenmore and his companion, there was a vapid-looking youth, flushed with wine, and playing recklessly, one of the gilded fools who was racing through an inherited fortune as fast as he could, a girl with him who shrieked music-hall from head to foot, and who seemed to be advising her befuddled companion as to his play.

The fifth member of the party was a man of uncertain age and dusky skin, whom Yvonne immediately placed as some princely potentate from abroad learning his first lesson in the game of civilised robbery.

The crowd was not unlike that which she expected to see, for she knew as well as any experienced gambler what is the chief purpose of a private room for high play. There the victims may be fleeced far more safely and with much greater profit than in the more public apartments.

Evidently the attendant to whom she had spoken had made the mistake of classing her as an easy victim, for she felt sure that otherwise she would hardly have received permission to play.

So, with a little inward smile, she determined to pose as such. The five players scarcely glanced at her as she approached the table, so intent were they on the game, and after watching a few turns by the dealer, she opened her purse and pushed one of the five-hundred-pound notes across to him.

He swept it into the bank, and with deft fingers counted out ten fifties, which he pushed towards her.

By watching the others, Yvonne had seen that the minimum stake was fifty pounds, while most of the players were staking far more on each turn.

She tossed a fifty on the seven, and "buttoned" it to lose; then another on the ace to win, and waited for the call. Surreptitiously she gazed at Bob Fenmore. That he was completely in the grip of the fever was plain. His cheeks were flushed with hectic spots, and his eyes were sparkling naturally. That he was playing some system of his own and losing at it was evident, for he was staking methodically in hundreds—five separate bets to a turn.

His companion was not betting, but was either advising him or cautioning him, Yvonne could not tell which. But she was whispering in his ear almost continuously. Then the next call came—the five won, and the seven lost, and for her fifty on the seven Yvonne received another fifty.

She left her original stake, and as the race had not yet been called, her bet on it still stood. Fenmore had backed the seven to win, but since it had lost, the hundred pounds he had put on it was swept into the bank. He had had no bet on the five, and putting another hundred on the seven to win, left his system as it had been. The dusky foreigner had lost on the five, and so had the gilded young fool. They, too, replenished their bets, and again the call was made.

So it continued for two tense hours, during which Yvonne played with varying luck, until at the end of that time she had lost over four hundred pounds. But during that time she had used her eyes to good purpose, and when a stop was made, while refreshments might be partaken of, she was in possession of the following facts.

Bob Fenmore, in the two hours play, had lost sixteen hundred pounds. The young fool who was rushing through a fortune had lost well over a thousand, while the dark-skinned man from abroad had lost his head towards the last, and by reckless play, had brought the total of his losses up to two thousand. The other women had wagered so very occasionally that their winnings or losses counted little beside the others; but Yvonne was under the impression that Marion Paul might have dropped some, while the other appeared to be a slight winner.

But the presence of Marion Paul there puzzled Yvonne more than a little. She knew a little about that successful young woman, and she did not strike Yvonne as the kind of person who was fool enough to drop much in the private room of a gambling club. She was much more likely to be on the other side of the fence, and as this thought came to Yvonne, a startling thing suggested itself to her.

But totalling the losses was not the only thing she had done during that two hours. She had watched the masked dealer almost continually, and for the past hour she had been firmly convinced that he was dealing a crooked game. In that case the players could never realise anything else but losses, and so brazen was the whole affair that the dealer did not even trouble to let his victims win occasionally.

An artist would have done so. And about that same dealer Yvonne was puzzled. There seemed to be a hint of something familiar about him, yet she failed utterly to place him. Still, she was sure she had seen him at some time or other. It was not that his features were familiar, or even his dress. It was simply an indefinable something, and so far she could not place it.

These thoughts kept passing through her mind whilst she partook of the extremely recherche supper which had been laid out on the buffet.

Fenmore ate feverishly, but his companion, Marion Paul, scarcely touched anything, contenting herself with a sandwich or two. His losses had apparently not affected the dark-skinned foreigner, for he munched away ravenously, and, between bites, attempted to carry on a conversation with Yvonne. She answered him in monosyllables, for her mind was busy.

The gilded young fool and his chorus-girl companion had retired to a divan in the corner, where she appeared to be consoling him over his losses. The dealer and the case-keeper had disappeared through a door behind the faro-table, probably to seek refreshment, too.

But at the end of half an hour they both returned and reseated themselves at the table. This was the signal for the others to make a move, and, after a preliminary skirmish for places, the game once more started. Yvonne played more cautiously, and by the simple method of backing in exactly the opposite way each card that Bob Fenmore played, she found that she was gradually making up her losses.

But she was the only one to do so, and from the frequent scowls cast in her direction by the dealer, she knew that he had spotted her method. The foreigner was playing more recklessly than ever, and his losses were becoming fearfully stiff. The youngster who was in tow of the chorus-girl had befuddled himself with too much wine, and his play was utterly maudlin.

It was all too plain now to Yvonne that the girl was simply a tout for the place, and would no doubt receive a substantial commission on the losses of the gilded victim. And the startling thought which Yvonne had had when she had surreptitiously watched the attitude of Marion Paul was this: Was that young lady only the agent of the gambling-den, and was she, perhaps, receiving a large sum to use her arts in keeping Bob Fenmore spurred on in the mad assault upon the demon of chance?

How little show of success that assault really had. Yvonne knew only too well, for the crookedness of the game was even more blatant than ever. And still she puzzled her brain and whipped up the settlings of memory to try and place the identity of the dealer. But when the end of the night's play came she was as far from guessing it as ever. But the next hour was to have some startling revelations for her.

The move to stop playing came first from Fenmore. He had been continuing his system since supper, but had lost with marvellous consistency, and by watching him closely, Yvonne knew that he stopped only because he was cleaned out. When he drew back, and turned away with a muttered imprecation, the dealer looked up and spoke suavely.

"A little loan, sir?" he said, in his husky tones. "You have had a bad run, but your luck may change."

Fenmore hesitated, then shook his head.

"No, thanks! I tried that last night, and fared worse then ever. I'll go home now. Are you ready, Marion"

Marion Paul smiled her assent, and as they turned away from the table Yvonne's surreptitious gaze was rewarded by seeing an unmistakable look of understanding pass between the music-hall star and the masked dealer. What could it mean?

And then, just at that moment, the dealer lifted his hand to his mask as though to adjust it, and, with a sharp thrill, Yvonne saw that his beard was false.

Mystery upon mystery! A crooked game, a disguised dealer, and masked at that. Her decision to disentangle the cloud of trouble which seemed to be brooding over her friend Marion Fenmore was leading her into strange places indeed, and the more puzzling became the maze, the more determined became Yvonne to follow it to its end.

The game broke up automatically when Bob Fenmore ceased playing, and Yvonne attracted no attention as she followed them from the room. The main faro-room beyond was empty, and likewise the front room. All the other devotees of the god Chance had evidently departed long since, and looking up at a clock over the door, Yvonne realised with a shock of surprise that it was past five o'clock in the morning.

She slipped into the wraps which an attendant held for her, and prolonged her departure until Bob Fenmore and Marion Paul had descended the stairs. The dusky foreigner had already gone, and just ahead of her the youngster hung sleepily on the arm of his companion. Thus Yvonne was really the last of the players to pass out into the cold, grey dawn.

She walked along for a short distance until she saw an early morning taxi approaching. This she hailed, and, leaning towards the driver, said:

"I want you to drive back into Milton Crescent, and go slowly until I tap on the window. When I do so, pull up and wait. I will tell you when I wish you to go on. And if anybody comes up to you, say you are waiting for a fare. I shall sit well back in the cab; as I do not wish to be seen. If you do this satisfactorily, I shall give you something over your ordinary tip."

The man touched his cap.

"I'll manage it all right, miss."

Then Yvonne entered the cab, which crept slowly round into the Crescent. It kept on running close to the kerb, until it had drawn past the house where the gambling had taken place. When it had reached a spot opposite the next house but one, Yvonne tapped sharply on the window, and the man stopped close to the kerb.

Then Yvonne twisted round, and through the pane of glass at the rear, began to keep watch on the house which held such interest for her. A quarter of an hour went by without anything happening which attracted her attention. At the end of that time, however, the door of the house opened, and on the crisp morning air Yvonne heard the shrill sound of a whistle. Somebody desired a taxi.

It was still so dark that it was impossible to see distinctly, but a few minutes later, when a taxi had turned the corner and drawn into the kerb, a figure descended the steps, and something in the set of the shoulders seemed strangely familiar to her.

As the other cab drew away from the kerb she softly lowered the window of the one in which she sat.

"As soon as that cab turns the corner, I want you to follow it," she said, in low tones. "Don't let it out of sight for a moment."

The driver nodded, and no sooner had the other disappeared than he turned sharply and started after it. Around the corner and up towards Hyde Park they went.

Leaning forward, Yvonne could see the other taxi just ahead, and when it turned down Piccadilly they were close behind it.

Reaching Dover Street, the front taxi turned up and drove on steadily until it had come almost to Grafton Street.

Then suddenly it drew into the curb, and of necessity Yvonne's driver was compelled to continue straight on. But she saw that he had wit enough to go as slowly as possible, and straining back she gazed tensely through the rear window. She saw the fare in the other cab descend, she saw him pay the driver. Then she saw him cross the pavement towards the entrance to some chambers, and as the light over the door fell upon his features she gave a startled gasp. It was the man who had dealt at the faro game back in Wilton Crescent. Of that cardinal fact she was positive. But now he was without his mask and beard. His features stood out in the glare of the light as the world knew them. They were the same features which the man walking with Marion Fenmore in Bond Street had borne.

They were the features of Harold Craig, the cousin of Bob Fenmore and the man with whose name gossip was connecting that of Marion Fenmore.

What had Yvonne stumbled upon? What could it all mean?

She leaned back for a moment in order to adjust her ideas to this new and startling development, then she put her head out of the window and told the man to drive to Queen Anne's Gate. And as she entered her apartments just as the crimson of morn was tinging the east, her chin was set with determination.

THE next day was a busy one for Yvonne. She did not even make a pretence of going to bed, but on arriving home disrobed and plunged at once into a cold bath. Then she dressed in a charming morning costume, went hastily through her letters before breakfast, and when Graves finally appeared was ready to sit down with him, looking as fresh as though she had retired at an early hour the night before.

Naturally he was curious to know what was the outcome of her expedition the previous evening, but to all his questions Yvonne presented a smiling refusal to enlighten.

"I suppose you did manage to get in to the place," he grunted, after several ineffectual attempts to discover what had happened. Yvonne laughed.

"I certainly did, uncle, and don't mind telling you that I found out a great deal more about Frileti's than I dreamed I should. But my discoveries were of such a nature that a complete readjustment of my ideas has become necessary, and, until I know exactly what will be the outcome of my plans, I must ask you to have patience."

And no more than that could he persuade her to say. After breakfast Yvonne prepared to go out, taking the precaution to put on a heavy veil. Then she sent for the car and told Alec to drive to an address in the City. It proved to be the office of a solicitor, and from its mustiness and general air of a past generation it seemed unlikely to be the sort of office which could handle the affairs of such an extremely modern young lady as Mademoiselle Yvonne. But she knew from past experience that old Jacob Frier, though passed by in the present strenuous days, was an invaluable man in some ways and more than once had he been of considerable use to her.

The old man himself received her, and when he saw whom it was his faded eyes lighted with pleasure.

Yvonne remained with him for less than half an hour in all, but before she left Jacob Frier had already put into motion the mysterious machinery which he controlled. And this same machinery would very quickly find out every detail to be known of a certain Harold Craig, Esq.

From there she drove through to Dover Street and, dismissing Alec, idled up and down in front of the shops for a considerable time, though had one taken the trouble to observe her closely it would have been discovered that never for a single second of the time was she out of sight of the chambers where her quarry had entered at daybreak that same morning.

But hour after hour passed and it was nearly noon before her patience was rewarded. Then, however, a tall figure issued forth from the chambers and stood negligently swinging a stick, while in response to the whistle of the commissionaire a taxi drove over from the stand on Hay Hill. It was the man she had seen the previous day in Bond Street with Marion Fenmore—Harold Craig.

She hailed a passing taxi herself and as he drove off he was once more followed though he did not know it. The chase proved to be a short one, for passing down Hay Hill his taxi went along Berkeley Street until it came to Piccadilly, up which it turned, keeping on towards Knightsbridge and stopping before an exclusive-looking private hotel.

There Craig descended and paying off the man entered the hotel.

Yvonne's taxi kept straight on. She knew as all the world knew that Marion Paul lived at the Hotel, and Harold Craig, the disguised faro dealer of Frileti's could be going there for no other purpose than to call upon the famous music-hall star.

The meaning glance which Yvonne's sharp eyes had intercepted in the faro room was proof enough of that. But what could it all mean? Were those two in league to lure Bob Fenmore to his ruin? Was Fenmore's friendship with Marion Paul only of her making? If so, what was she getting out of it? What had Craig been able to promise her to induce her to take a hand in such a risky game?

The price would have to be a high one to tempt Marion Paul. And exactly what was Craig's purpose? Was he still determined to marry Marion Fenmore? Did his defeat for her hand still rankle? Or was it all merely vengeance, and was Bob Fenmore the easy victim?

These and a dozen other questions Yvonne asked herself on the way through Kensington and across the park to Chelsea. But when the cab turned homewards and finally drew up at Queen Anne's Mansions she was no nearer a solution, though the tentative plan which had been stirring in her mind since the night before was now more firmly fashioned.

She lunched lightly and alone, for Graves had gone to the club. After lunch she smoked a thoughtful cigarette, after which she retired to her room and sought the rest she had missed the previous night. It was past six before she woke, and then it was only because of the persistent knocking of Anna, her maid, on the door of the room. In response to Yvonne's summons Anna entered bearing a thick envelope in her hand.

"I am sorry to have disturbed you, mademoiselle," she said, "but this letter came by hand a few moments ago, and as it was marked 'urgent' I thought you would wish to have it at once."

"You did quite right, Anna," replied Yvonne drowsily. "Let me see what it is."

She took the envelope, but when her eyes rested on the superscription she became suddenly wide awake. She knew it to be from old Jacob Frier, and that meant that he had already completed his investigations for he was not the man to send in half a report.

She did not attempt to investigate until she had dressed, but when tea was served she broke the seal of the envelope and took out the enclosed matter. It proved to be extremely comprehensive in the ground it covered, and before Yvonne had completely digested all of it evening had drawn in.

When she had finished she locked the report away in her desk and dressed for dinner. A 'phone message from the club conveyed the information that Graves was dining there, so Yvonne was alone.

She hurried through her after dinner cigarette and then once more prepared to go out. She had not altered the colour of her hair since the previous night, and the only thing she took this night which she had not had before was a small automatic.

It was just on the stroke of nine when Alec drove round with the car, and hurrying out Yvonne told him to drive to Wilton Crescent. She descended at Frileti's, and although the man at the door looked surprised at her early appearance, he recognised her from the night before and offered no objections to letting her in. She went at once to the floor above where a maid took her things.

"You are rather early, madam," she ventured. "I am afraid you will be compelled to wait for an hour yet before there is any play."

Yvonne nodded carelessly. "I came early on purpose." she said. "I wish to see the proprietor. Do you know if he is about?"

"He usually arrives about half past nine, madam, but I am afraid he will refuse to see you. It is one of his rules not to interview clients."

"He will see me I think when he knows the purpose of my visit," rejoined Yvonne. "Tell him that the lady who played in the private faro room last evening wishes to see him on a matter which is of the utmost importance to himself."

"Very well, madam, I will go and tell him."

The attendant slipped away at once, and while she waited Yvonne strolled through the silent gaming rooms, carelessly examining the tables and fittings.

Some twenty minutes passed before the attendant returned, but when she did she conveyed the information that the proprietor would give Yvonne a ten minute interview in the private faro room where she had played the night before.

Yvonne nodded her thanks and made her way straight to the room. Opening the door she stepped inside, and seated at the table exactly as he had been when she first saw him was the bearded and masked dealer whom she now knew to be none other than Harold Craig. He peered through the eyeholes of the mask at her as she entered but made no remark. He was evidently puzzled as to why she wanted to see him, and was determined that she should start the ball rolling. Yvonne was nothing loth.

"It is only natural to presume that you are wondering why I have sought an interview," she said coolly, "so I shall come straight to the point. In a word I wish to know how much you will take to sell?"

"To sell!" he echoed in amazement. "To sell what?"

"Frileti's, of course. I wish to buy your rights here."

"But, my dear madam, I do not wish to sell Frileti's at any price. If that is why you wished to see me I am afraid you have but wasted your time."

"I don't think so," responded Yvonne evenly. "I repeat that I wish to buy and am willing to pay a reasonable price. I think that on consideration you will decide to sell."

For the first time the masked man at the faro table seemed to get a hint of some deeper meaning behind his visitor's remarks. There seemed to be almost the hint of a threat in her last sentence.

"I am afraid I don't understand," he said finally. "Why should I decide to sell?"

Yvonne made no immediate answer, but bending slightly she opened her bag and took out a thick roll of notes.

"There are ten thousand pounds," she said tossing them on the table. "That is what I am prepared to give you for Frileti's, and I think you will take it."

The man laughed abruptly.

"You are pleased to be facetious," he said. "Do you know that the place is worth at least fifty thousand?"

Yvonne shrugged.

"I have no doubt it is the way you run it," she replied curtly.

"What do you mean," he snapped, bending forward.

"I mean exactly what I say. I played here last night and not being a fool saw the kind of faro you dealt. There wasn't a single player at the table had the ghost of a chance. It was the most blatant robbery I ever saw. That is why you will sell to me at my price. If you don't— well the police would be delighted to know that Frileti's had reopened."

"So you are a stool pigeon, are you?" he snarled.

"Not at all," she replied coolly. "Were I that I shouldn't be offering you ten thousand cash for the place. You are quite mistaken. I can see a fortune to be made here, and since I have been clever enough to read your game I can force you to sell."

For a time the other was silent then he looked up.

"Look here," he said. "Supposing I were to say that you had the advantage of me and that I was willing to take you into partnership for that ten thousand, what would you say?"

"That would require some thought," replied Yvonne slowly. "If you make it a definite offer I will give you a definite answer."

"I do make it a definite offer."

"Then I think I am prepared to accept it on one condition."

"What is that?"

"It is that I shall do the dealing in this room."

"Impossible. That is the one thing which I insist on doing myself."

"Then I am afraid I must revert to the first offer I made you. Unless you grant me that I shall certainly not consider a partnership."

"But I have a particular reason for dealing in this room."

"And so have I. Perhaps my reason is as strong as yours."

He looked at her sharply.

"What do you mean?"

Yvonne shrugged.

"I haven't the remotest intention of telling you," she said. "But this I will say. If your purpose is not carried out by me, then at the end of a week, I shall withdraw and let you do the dealing here."

"But how can you say that when you don't know my reason?" he objected.

"I can only presume it is the fleecing of those who play here," she answered, "and as I shall fleece them all that should satisfy you."

"Do you know enough about dealing a game of faro to do it safely?" he asked.

"I can do it more smoothly than you did it last night," she rejoined. "Come, we have talked enough! Do you take me as a partner, or do you sell on my terms? It is quite immaterial to me which you do. But one or the other I certainly intend shall be done."

"Will you tell me your name?" he asked. "I don't know you."

"Nor I you," she replied. "And I do not think names are necessary. I shall pay you ten thousand pounds here and now. In return, you give me a receipt and a promise to pay me half of the profits. A name doesn't matter. I am not afraid that I shall not be paid."

The man sat in silence for a long time. There was no question but that he was trying to make up his mind to refuse, but at last he spread out his hands in surrender, and Yvonne knew that her bluff had gone through.

And so that evening when the few players arrived in the private room they found, not the usual masked, bearded dealer, but handling the silver-dealing box the mysterious young woman who had played the night before.

Fenmore came again in company with Marion Paul. It was evident that in some way Craig had conveyed the news of the change to her, for she showed no signs of surprise on entering. Fenmore seemed rather pleased than otherwise, remarking that perhaps a change of dealers meant a change of luck.

The dusky foreigner did not come until later, when the play was in full progress, though the youngster and his chorus girl companion were there early.

Yvonne dealt the game in finished style, and if Harold Craig had been an adept at rooking the players she went him one better.

Fenmore had come well provided with money as usual, but when the pause came for supper he was out even more than he had been at the same hour the night before. It was while they were consuming the refreshments that the door opened, and none other than Craig himself entered. But he came not with the mask and beard he had worn at the table. He was quite undisguised, and had entered as an ordinary client. It was quite evident that he never dreamed his unknown partner had guessed his identity. He nodded in a friendly fashion to his cousin, and shook hands with Marion Paul, but beyond that paid them no attention.

After supper he took a hand in the game, and it gave the new dealer an ironical pleasure to fleece him as she was fleecing the others. Yet it was obvious to Yvonne that he had come as he had merely to see if she were doing as she had promised, while Fenmore seemed to think that Craig had come to spy on him.

He stayed scarcely an hour, however; but, as usual, the others continued play until morning. Nor was that night any different from the others. Every player lost heavily, but none more so than Bob Fenmore.

And so things continued for another week, until one morning when Bob Fenmore staggered out of the place Yvonne knew that he would never return. Every penny of his wife's money had gone where his own had gone. Craig was there on that last night, and they departed together. Now Yvonne's purpose was accomplished, as she thought, and when the last player had gone she drove back to Queen Anne's Gate, with a sigh of relief.

"Thank goodness that is over!" she murmured. "This afternoon I shall go to see Marion Fenmore and give into her own hands the money I have fleeced from Bob."

But many things were to happen before that afternoon, and those things had their beginning when Craig went home with Fenmore. They drove straight to the house in the quiet square, where only Bayles was up waiting for his master. Fenmore led the way to the library and poured himself out a drink. Then he turned savage, bloodshot eyes on his cousin.

"What do you want to say to me?" he snapped. "If you have come to preach, you may as well save your breath. I know exactly what I have done, and that I have only myself to thank for it all. If it is any satisfaction to you to know it, I can tell you that last night finishes me. I haven't a penny left in the world. Marion's is gone as well as my own."

Craig adopted a conciliatory manner.

"I didn't come to preach," he said, "nor did I go to Frileti's to spy on you, as you seem to think. Remember, I am a loser as well as yourself. What I came to say was this: If you are broke, I can let you have something if you need it."

Fenmore laughed harshly.

"No, thanks. I wouldn't borrow money from you, Harold, at any price. But you can do one thing for me—you can get out and leave me in peace."

At that moment there was a knock on the door, and Bayles entered with an early morning edition.

"I brought the paper in, sir," he said. "There is serious news."

"What is it, Bayles?"

"War has been declared with Germany, sir."

Bob Fenmore set his drink down and took the paper quickly. Opening it at the news page he ran his eye over the paragraph which told that Britain had at last become embroiled in long-expected world war. He read every word without remark, then he tossed the paper across to Craig and walked to the window. Then suddenly, while the other was still engrossed with the paper, Fenmore turned back to the desk. Seating himself, he drew forward a sheet of writing-paper, and picking up a pen began to write swiftly. Less than a single sheet covered, then taking up an envelope he addressed it with a single name—Marion." That done, he folded the note thrust it in the envelope, and sealed it.

"Look here," he said, swinging round in his chair, "you said you would be glad to help me, Harold."

Craig threw the paper aside, and nodded.

"Certainly."

"Well, you can," went on Fenmore, "but not in the way you think I mean. You see this note?"

"Yes."

"It is addressed, as you see, to my wife. I want you to see that she gets it as soon as she comes down."

"Can't you give it to her yourself?"

"I shall not be here—and there comes the second part of what you can do for me. As you already know, I am cleaned out. There is absolutely nothing left in the shape of money. But there is one thing which I have not touched—and will not touch. That is the Fenmore necklace. It is worth about ten thousand, and I want Marion to realise on it."

"But what are you going to do?"

"Will you pass me your word of honour that under no circumstance will you reveal what I tell you?"

"Certainly."

"When I came into the house this morning I hadn't the faintest idea what to do. To tell you the truth, I had made up my mind to take the only obvious way out, but since reading the paper I have changed my mind."

"You mean?"

"I intend to enlist and go to the front as soon as possible. It will be my one desire to get into the thick of it, because when I am gone my life insurance will pay back what I have taken of Marion's. And for a year, at least, the amount she realises on the necklace will be sufficient to support her."

"Do you really mean this?"

"I was never more serious in my life. Now, will you pass your word to keep mum, and do what you can to advise Marion. I—I have been a beast, and now that it is too late I see what I have done. But there is no use whining now. I made my own bed and must lie on it, only—only—oh, but what is the use? Tell me, Craig, will you do as I ask?"

"I will do what you ask."

"Your word?"

"My word."

Fenmore gave a sigh.

"Then I shall rest easier. Poor little girl, I am afraid I have made her frightfully unhappy, and she will be well rid of me." He rose as he spoke, and approached the door.

"I am going to change," he said. "Wait until I come down."

When he had disappeared, Craig walked to the window and stood looking out. Only now that he was alone did he allow the triumph he felt to reveal itself.

"Gad, but the fates are working with me!" he muttered. "To think that war should be declared just as his last penny was gone! There was nothing for him to do but what he said. This, however, is better—much better. If I am any judge of the situation, he will stand little chance of coming back from this war. It will be the greatest slaughter in history, and in the mood he will be in he will plunge straight into the thick of it. Then Marion will be mine. I wonder what he wrote to her. I must manage to read it before I give it to her."

And in this fashion did Craig commune with himself until the door opened to admit Fenmore. He was now clad in a rough tweed suit and cap, and in his hand carried a small leather case. This he passed to Craig.

"That is the necklace," he said curtly. "See that Marion has it with the letter. And remember, Harold, I hold you responsible for what I have asked of you. Good-bye!"

Craig shook hands with him.

"Don't you think you ought to change your mind, Bob?" he said. "Let me make you a loan, and then you can make a new start."

"I told you I would accept nothing from you—and I won't!" replied Fenmore. "If you do what I have asked of you, it will be sufficient. I am not fit to touch Marion's feet, and she is well rid of me."

He turned as he spoke, and took a long look at the room which had been his favourite den for so many years; then, not daring to trust himself further, he stumbled from the room, his eyes blinded with a sudden mist. The door closed, then came the slamming of the front door, and Craig knew that at last he had won. Bob Fenmore had been swept from his path, and had gone forth to what seemed certain death, leaving his home and Marion.

No sooner was he sure that Fenmore had really gone than Craig took up the leather case and pressed the spring. The lid flew up, and there was revealed the famous Fenmore necklace.

There was no doubt but that it would fetch a large sum.

But Craig had no intention that Marion should receive that sum. Only by her utter dependence on him could he control each thread of the future. He laid the case back on the desk, then took up the letter which Fenmore had addressed to her. Coolly breaking the seal, Craig unfolded the sheet of paper, and read what was written. And as he scanned the contents a daring plan came to him. The note ran as follows:

"Marion,—I am going out of your life for ever, and in due course you will probably hear of my death. I am making all arrangements with my solicitors that you should. I am utterly cleaned out, and beyond the necklace which accompanies this there is nothing to leave you. Forgive my action, and forget me. I know too late that I love you more than all. My gambling was madness, but what is done is done.

Try to think kindly of me sometimes. BOB."

Craig nodded thoughtfully.

"It will do as it is. Thank fortune their names are the same. And when Marion Paul appears wearing the Fenmore necklace I think London will sit up. And who can question it when she has a letter like this in her possession? I think that this will be the last straw, and if it doesn't force Marion Fenmore into doing my wishes, then I am very much mistaken. Yes, Craig, my boy, I think your luck is certainly in. Ah, I think I hear Marion's voice in the hall! I must get these out of sight."

He hurriedly stuffed the letter and case in his pocket, and as the door opened went to meet Marion Fenmore, who stood there looking for all the world like a hunted fawn.

End of Prologue.

THE STORY.

THE GAMBLING DEN—AND AFTER.

Yvonne witnesses (1) the entry of Robert Fenmore and Mariah Paul to the gambling room, and (2) the unmasking of the disguised dealer.

The First Chapter.   The Murder of Harold Craig.

SEPTEMBER, October, and November had slipped away, and the crisp, cold days of December had come. The terrible struggle which was raging on the Continent was still, and would continue to be, the all-absorbing topic of conversation to the majority of people, and happenings which in ordinary times would have created quite a ripple on the surface of society were now passed over with scarcely a comment.

Since the magnificent action of the British troops at Mons the people of the Empire had begun to realise that the struggle upon which we had embarked was to be no sinecure, and, with their usual capacity for tackling a stern proposition, had girded up their loins so to speak, and were all intent on supplying the men and money necessary to bring the war to a successful issue.

But in the backwaters of Clubland, where Bob Fenmore had been well known, men still occasionally referred to his mysterious disappearance back in August, just about the time war had been declared. Few facts had ever become known of this, and in the greater interest of the war the usual enterprising reporter had not ferreted out the mass of news which otherwise would have been the case.

A few isolated paragraphs only had been devoted to the matter, and the bulk of those had contained little information. They had said that Fenmore had disappeared, and that his whereabouts were unknown. And that was practically all.

His friends, however, knew that shortly after his disappearance Marion Fenmore had given up the house which had been theirs and had moved into a flat in Knightsbridge. Of course, gossip had it that Fenmore had gone through every penny of her money as well as his own, and had left her in a very precarious financial position. Some there were who smiled slyly and spoke of Harold Craig; but, strange to say, from the first day of Bob Fenmore's disappearance, he had gone no more to the house to see Fenmore's wife. And only Marion Fenmore and himself knew that she had sent him away and had requested him never to return. But not even Craig knew where Marion Fenmore got the money which was necessary to carry on her home. He little dreamed that his dismissal and Marion's independence were both due to a letter which had reached her on the afternoon of her husband's disappearance, and which, with what it had held, had made her independent of his plans. That letter had been as follows:

"Enclosed you will find forty banknotes for one thousand pounds each. This money represents a portion of the sum which your husband lost in gaming. Had he lost it in a straight game the writer would have done nothing in the matter. But it was stolen from him most flagrantly, and therefore the writer is returning it for your sake, and in order to foil the schemes of those who robbed him. The one condition imposed is that you invest it and keep it in your own name, not permitting your husband to touch it until he has come to his senses. And the writer would also suggest that you dismiss from your circle of friends your husband's cousin. Nothing but trouble can ever come from that quarter. Do not hesitate to accept the money enclosed. It is really your own. One day, perhaps, the identity of the writer will be revealed to you, and then you will understand."

It had been typewritten on plain paper, and had contained nothing which would indicate the source from which it had come. Of course, had the notes been traced, some light might have been thrown on the matter, but when Marion Fenmore had realised that her husband had really gone, she had lost interest in everything about her, and had sent the notes to her bank.

One thing she did do, however, and that was to send Harold Craig from the house as she had been advised, and from that day forth she had scarcely ventured from her new home. Something had stopped within her when she had realised the truth, and now she could no more face the world with a smiling face when her heart was bleeding. But gossip had been consoled with a new bone, for of late Craig was to be seen almost constantly with Marion Paul, the music-hall star.

And so the weeks had slipped by, letting the Fenmore scandal and such things slip back into the swamp of forgetfulness. But the whole subject was to come up again, and in such a startling manner that it was to receive almost as much attention as the news from the front. One thing which should be mentioned, and which Fenmore's friends had never forgotten or forgiven, was his apparent callousness towards his wife; for on the very night of his disappearance, Marion Paul had appeared on the stage wearing the famous Fenmore necklace, and rumour had it that just before dropping out of sight, Bob Fenmore had written her an affectionate letter, telling her it was his last gift to her. If that were true, as it certainly seemed to be, then he must be the scoundrel he was said to be. Then about the middle of

December, London was electrified to read of the murder of Harold Craig, and the interest of the affair was materially increased by the utter mystery which surrounded it. Very few facts were known, and the gist of those were as follows:

On the night of the murder, Marion Paul had gone to the theatre as usual, accompanied by her maid. During the evening, Harold Craig had called at her flat, and had let himself in with a key she had given him to use that evening. The actress was giving a small supper after the theatre, and Craig had volunteered to go to the flat and see that things were arranged for their arrival. Hence his possession of the key. The porter of the building had seen him enter about ten o'clock and had seen him go up in the lift to the apartment. He had been alone.

Shortly after eleven, Marion Paul and half a dozen friends had arrived, and had gone up by way of the stairs, since the lift was not large enough for the whole party. On entering the flat the gentlemen—three—had left their things in the hall, while the ladies had gone with their hostess into her boudoir.

The maid had preceded the men to the sitting-room, but no sooner had she entered than she had uttered a loud scream and had rushed back. The foremost of the men had caught her, and the others, pushing forward, had been shocked to see the body of a man lying huddled up near the large table in the centre of the room, while the room itself was in great disorder. They had hurried forward and picked him up, but only when they had laid him on the couch did they see that it was Harold Craig. His face was terribly swollen and distorted, and all efforts to revive him failed.

It was when there was no doubt about his being dead that one of the men had gone to break the news to Marion Paul. She had appeared greatly affected at first, but after a little had become calmer. Then the police and a doctor had been sent for, and Marion Paul with her maid had removed to a nearby hotel for the night.

It was obvious that murder had been committed, though how had not yet been decided. The doctor had at first been under the impression that the unfortunate man had died of an epileptic attack, but a more detailed examination had shown that he was the victim of a poison of some kind. But what kind, or how it had been administered, was as yet unknown.

That there had been a violent struggle before he had succumbed seemed evident from the condition of the room, and when a careful examination had been made by the police, they had discovered one thing which seemed to give a slight clue. This was a window at the rear of the flat which looked out on some outbuildings at the rear. The catch showed plainly that it had been forced, and by way of the outbuildings, an active person could gain access to the flat without much trouble.

The general impression was that the murderer must have been a man of some strength, for Craig had been no weakling, and had put up a stiff resistance before he gave in.

The one thing which mostly puzzled the police on the night of the murder was the motive. Although the room was in such disorder, nothing appeared to be missing, and not a single thing seemed to have been taken from the pockets of the dead man. His money, his cigarette and card-case, his keys, watch, and a small sovereign-case were all intact. But on the morning after the murder, when the body had been removed and Marion Paul had returned to the flat, she discovered, on opening the small safe in the sitting-room, that the combination had been forced and something of great value taken. That something was the famous Fenmore necklace. *But several other cases containing jewels had been left untouched.*

A thorough inventory of her possessions had shown that this was the only thing which was missing. Strange to say, the night of the murder had been almost the only night for weeks past that she had not worn the necklace, and this evident knowledge on the part of the murderer but widened the circle of mystery. And it was this entry of the Fenmore necklace into the mystery which had caused more public interest than even the murder itself. After the inventory, Marion Paul had collected a few belongings and had gone back to the hotel where she had spent the previous night, leaving the flat once more in the possession of the police. These things, and these things only, did the public know. If any further facts had been discovered, or if anyone had come under suspicion, the police had kept the information to themselves.

•   •   •   •   •

On the morning after the murder of Harold Craig, Sexton Blake sat at breakfast in his Baker Street apartments, reading the newspaper reports of the crime with no little interest. He had scarcely finished them, and betaken himself to the consulting-room, when Mrs. Bardell entered to announce that Inspector Thomas of Scotland Yard had called. The inspector himself followed close on her heels, and Blake welcomed him warmly, for it had been some little time since he had seen him.

"Well, inspector, how are things?" he asked, indicating a chair and passing over the cigars.

The inspector lit the weed and puffed thoughtfully for a moment before replying.

"I can't complain of things in general," he said finally. "The only trouble is that I have so much to do that I scarcely know where to begin."

"Hence your early morning call upon me, I presume," laughed Blake. "But if that is the reason, inspector, let me warn you that I am in the same predicament myself. Both Tinker and I have been going night and day."

"I know, Blake; but I have come to see you on a matter which you simply must help me with if possible."

"You know I will do that, inspector. But tell me what it is."

"Have you read this morning's papers?"

"Of course."

"Then you will have read of the murder case."

"I just finished doing so, when you arrived. Rather an unfortunate affair."

"It is that," remarked the inspector slowly. "Did you form any theory at all when reading it?"

Blake laughed.

"You know I am not as precipitate as that, inspector. Have you?"

"Well, I have and I haven't. Since you have read the reports in the papers, it is unnecessary for me to go into detail. But I will outline all the facts I know, and then, if you can spare the time, I should like to have you come round and have a look at the place."

"Go ahead, I am listening."

"Well, if you read the report in the 'Daily Echo,' you will have the facts about as they are, though there are some things that the reporters haven't got hold of, and we don't propose they shall."

"Ah, that sounds more interesting!"

"You noted, of course, that the Fenmore necklace which Marion Paul had, appeared to be the motive of the affair?"

"Yes."

"Well, what does that suggest to you?"

"It suggests, naturally, that the perpetrator of the crime may have entered the place primarily for the purpose of theft and not for murder. We can suppose that he became possessed of the information that Marion Paul was not wearing the necklace last night, and thinking it would be in the flat, entered for the purpose of stealing it. Then he was surprised by finding Craig there, and after a struggle overcame the latter, and to be on the safe side, killed him."

"Exactly. But how do you suggest that he may have known the necklace was not being worn last night?"

"Why, he may have gone to the theatre, and seeing that Marion Paul hadn't it on, took a chance of finding it at her flat. A thief who had made up his mind to steal it, might go to the theatre night after night until he saw her without it."

"True. I never thought of that."

"For goodness' sake, inspector, don't take it as a definite theory. I was simply telling you what a superficial reading of the newspaper reports suggested."

"I understand that; but it is always interesting to hear you theorise. Now, then, Blake, I will tell you what the newspapers do not know. Marion Paul has told us something which seems to point to the real motive, and also to indicate the possible identity of the perpetrator."

"Ah, now you are really interesting, inspector!"

"You will think so when I finish. This morning, after she had discovered the loss of the Fenmore necklace, I had a long talk with her and drew her out. I finally got her to loosen her tongue a little, and the sum and substance of what she suggested was this. She thinks the entry to the flat was made by no casual thief, but that it was a carefully-planned attempt to gain possession of the Fenmore necklace. She thinks, however, that the murder was not premeditated, but was the outcome of the finding of Craig in the place. And she thinks the thief went to the lengths he did out of motives of revenge."

"Revenge!" echoed Blake. "What do you mean?"

"She seems to think that the missing Robert Fenmore could tell us something about the events of last night, if we could find him."

"Good heavens, does she suspect Bob Fenmore of murdering his cousin?"

"She doesn't say so in so many words, but she hints that such might be the case, and strengthens her theory by saying that during the past two months she has had more than one threatening letter from an anonymous source which she thought was Fenmore. She hinted that he was jealous of Craig's attention to her. You remember the talk about Fenmore and Marion Paul just before he disappeared, and the scandal there was when she appeared wearing the Fenmore necklace while Fenmore's wife had to move to cheaper quarters?"

"Oh, I heard all the gossip," replied Blake, "but I never believed half of it. I knew Fenmore slightly, and although he certainly made a fool of himself I never could believe he was a cad or a crook. At the same time, Marion Paul's tale put him in a very bad light."

"Well, Marion Paul showed me the letter she received from him when he sent her the necklace. It was certainly given to her all right. But let me tell you the sequel to the suggestions she made. I went out early this morning to Knightsbridge where Mrs. Fenmore has taken a flat. I wanted to see her and ask her if she had any idea of the whereabouts of her husband. I was shown into a small sitting-room, and after waiting for a few minutes a nurse appeared and told me that Mrs. Fenmore could not see me as she was very ill. I was about to go when on a side table I noticed a small leather case which aroused my curiosity. I got rid of the nurse on the pretence that I wanted to see Mrs. Fenmore's own maid, and while she was gone from the room I opened the case I had seen. What do you think it was?"

"What?"

"It was the Fenmore necklace which was stolen last night from the safe in Marion Paul's sitting-room."

For once Blake was visibly startled.

"Good heavens!" he ejaculated. "Is that a fact?"

"It is."

"What did you do about it?"

"What could I do? I closed the case just as the maid entered the room, and giving her some sort of message for the mistress made my way out. But in my opinion that incident strengthens the suspicion against Robert Fenmore and I shall do my best to find him. At the same time I should be glad if you would come along to the flat and make an examination there."

"I shall do so with pleasure, inspector."

Blake rose as he spoke and entering the dressing-room got his hat and coat, for it was a cold, foggy day outside. Then he signified his readiness and together they departed. Hailing a taxi the inspector gave the address of Marion Paul's flat, and on the way Blake asked a few incidental questions regarding the condition of the place, eliciting the information that everything had been left absolutely untouched.

Two of the inspector's plain clothes men were on guard, one at the rear of the flat and one in the sitting-room where the tragedy had taken place. As the inspector had said, the room had been left as it was when the discovery had been made. The flat itself was not a large one but was conveniently laid out and beautifully furnished.

Immediately on entering there was a small, square hall, which had been converted into a sort of lounge. Immediately to the left of this was a small boudoir off which opened a large bed-room. Further down the hall, and also to the left was the large sitting-room where the tragedy had taken place.

No pains had been spared in the decorating and furnishing of this room.

From the rich curtains over the window to the fine ormolu table and desk of the Italian Renaissance it was most sumptuous. At first glance it struck one as being in the wildest disorder, thus conveying the impression that a terrific struggle had taken place.

But Blake completed his survey of the whole flat before returning to a more detailed examination of the sitting-room.

Beyond the sitting-room, and at the end of the main hall, was the dining-room. There the hall turned to the right, and on the left again was a small smoking-room. Opposite this was another bed-room, and further along on the right the maid's room.

Across the hall was the ordinary bath-room and then, some distance down, at the end of the hall, the kitchen and domestic offices.

Blake finished his survey at the kitchen, and walking to the window gazed through it at the out-buildings, by way of which it was thought the murderer had come. Then he turned and made his way back to the sitting-room. Standing at the door he gazed carefully about him before entering. Slowly his gaze swept the windows, the walls, the ceiling, the floor and the different objects in the room. Then he entered and walked straight to the small safe which stood in a corner of the room. It was of American make and opened by means of a numbered combination of nickel.

Blake knelt in front of it and turned the handle, finding that it had been left unlocked for the police.

"Did you find any fingerprints?" he asked of the inspector who was standing beside him.

"Yes—several. I took copies of them and sent them to the Yard to be photographed. I left orders for the proofs to be sent on here as soon as they were ready, and I expect they will arrive before long."

"Good. That simplifies matters somewhat."

As he spoke Blake drew open the door of the safe and gazed at the interior. There was little of interest there, however, for already Marion Paul had removed most of the contents, and those which remained were only a few unimportant papers.

After a cursory glance Blake closed the door and returned to the other side of the room. Here he dropped to the floor, and on his hands and knees began to go over the carpet inch by inch. The inspector had pointed out to him the exact spot where the body of the murdered man had been found, and not until he reached that spot did Blake draw out his pocket glass. Then he bent close to the floor, and blocking out the area before him in dozens of imaginary squares, began to closely scrutinise every inch. At the end of about ten minutes he raised his head.

"The carpet seems damp just here, inspector. Do you know the reason?"

"Miss Paul said that when she left for the theatre last evening there was a vase of roses on the table. When they returned and discovered what had happened the vase and the flowers were on the floor near Craig. Evidently the vase had been knocked off the table during the struggle, and the water had become absorbed by the carpet. That is the vase on the table, just over your head."

Blake turned and gazed at the object which the inspector pointed out. It was a tall glass of ordinary pattern containing a small amount of water in the bottom.

"What became of the roses it contained?" asked Blake suddenly.

The inspector shrugged.

"I am not certain, but I think they were thrown out."

Then Blake turned to the plain clothes man who stood by the door.

"I wish you would go to the kitchen and ask your mate if he knows what became of the flowers which were taken from this room. If they are in the dust box you might bring them to me."

As the man saluted and departed the inspector turned to Blake with a puzzled look.

"What on earth do you want of those flowers?" he asked.

Blake shook his head.

"I simply want to examine every object which was in the room when the murder took place," he replied. "They should never have been removed."

"I didn't take them out," rejoined the inspector. "Either Miss Paul or her maid did so."

Blake nodded without replying and went back to his work. Passing the damp spot on the carpet he began to circuit the table, when suddenly he bent forward quickly and picked up something which lay beneath the folds of the table cover. He glanced round to see if the inspector was observing him, but finding that he had strolled across to the window Blake thrust the object he had found into his pocket, then he proceeded.

Over every inch of the floor he went until he had worked his way back to the door, then he thrust the pocket glass away and rose to his feet. Strolling slowly about the room he began to remark casually on each object within it, much after the fashion of an expert passing judgment on the contents of a room which were for sale.

"Terrible disorder," he murmured half aloud, while the inspector gazed at him in puzzlement. "Fine pictures, mostly autographed, quite uninjured. Several ordinary ornaments of the mantel knocked over and some broken, but the most valuable objects there fortunately uninjured. Desk the same— fittings scattered about the floor but nothing of value injured. Pictures all askew on the table, but beyond the vase, which is unbroken, nothing seems to have been knocked off. Several antique ornaments scattered about, and nearly all the draperies in disorder, but no serious damage done.

"The room presents every indication of a terrible struggle having taken place, but it is a remarkable thing that so little actual damage has been done. Half an hour's work would set the room quite to rights again. And it is an extraordinary thing that the vase on the table was not broken when it fell to the floor, because it is of thin glass. Still, it is remarkable what a tall glass objects will stand sometimes without breaking. It depends on how they hit, I suppose. H'm."

As he finished his monologue he turned towards the door where the plain clothes man was standing.

"Well?" inquired Blake.

"I asked the other man if he knew what had become of the flowers, sir," he said, "and he tells me that the maid burnt them in the kitchen stove this morning."

"Ah, that is a pity. However, it doesn't matter much."

It was obvious that for some time past the inspector had been anxious to have Blake's opinion, and now he could contain his impatience no longer.

"What do you think of it?" he asked. "Do you agree with my theory?"

"You mean the one inspired by what Marion Paul told you?"

"Yes."

"Well, frankly inspector, I don't care to make a definite statement just at present. I should like to have a look at the premises at the rear and then give the thing some thought. I prefer to form my theory independent of anything suggested by Marion Paul. Women are so apt to be carried away by their emotions when under stress, and I am not so sure anyway that I think much of Miss Paul's opinion."

At that moment there was a warning cough from the plain clothes man at the door, and turning, Blake saw a tall, heavily-veiled figure in black standing at the door. She lifted her veil at that moment and he saw that it was none other than Marion Paul herself. She must have overheard every word he said. The inspector hurried forward to her.

"Good morning, Miss Paul," he said solicitously. "We didn't hear you come in."

"Good morning, Inspector Thomas," she said, in rich clear tones. "I must apologise if I intruded upon any examination. I wished to get one or two things which my maid forgot to pack so came along and used my own key to come in."

"Oh, no, indeed," the inspector hastened to assure her. "Let me introduce Mr. Sexton Blake. I thought he would be professionally interested in this case, so brought him along to see what he made of it."

Marion Paul bowed in acknowledgment of the introduction.

"I have heard a great deal of Mr. Blake," she said. "His opinion should be of great interest."

"You flatter me," murmured Blake. "I am afraid I have not yet formed any opinion."

"And evidently do not think much of mine," she laughed; but with a momentary glint of something else in her eyes which Blake's sharp gaze noted, although the inspector did not notice it.

"I must apologise for my remarks," said Blake, also smiling. "I am afraid they were ungallant to the opposite sex."

"And you really don't think my suspicions are correct?" she persisted.

"Oh, I didn't say that," answered Blake, a trifle curtly. "I said that before accepting the theory which the inspector had formed after hearing your story that I preferred to complete my examination of the place. It is quite probable that I shall arrive at the same theory by a different method. Were that the case it would but strengthen it."

"I see," she nodded. "Then you have not yet finished?"

"No. There is yet the rear of the place where the entry was forced."

"Ah, then I shall not detain you. I shall get what I came for and go at once."

They stood aside while she walked to the desk and opening one of the drawers took out a small leather writing case. Then she closed the drawer and turned towards the door. Just as she reached it Blake spoke.

"By the way, Miss Paul, Inspector Thomas told me that you showed him the letter which Robert Fenmore had sent to you with the Fenmore necklace. Would you permit me to see it also?"

She hesitated for a moment and glanced at him sharply.

"Really, Mr. Blake, if you are only here out of professional curiosity I don't see why I should show you things which are essentially of a private nature."

Blake bowed, but as he bent his head darted a look at the inspector. The latter evidently read it rightly, for he turned towards Marion Paul and said:

"But I am in hopes that Mr. Blake will give me his assistance in the case, Miss Paul. I am very busy at the present time, and I am sure if Mr. Blake does take on the case he will ferret out the truth speedily."

"Oh, in that case I will show him the letter," she said, with heightened colour.

She seated herself at once, and, opening the case, took out an envelope. This she handed to Blake. The latter took it and lifted the flap, noting as he did so that the envelope was both unaddressed and unsealed. Then he spread out the sheet of paper which it contained, and glanced through the note which Bob Fenmore had written on the morning he had disappeared, and which he had intended for his wife. When he had finished he folded it up again and calmly thrust it in his pocket.

"I shall examine this a little later, and have the pleasure of returning it to you later in the day, Miss Paul," he said coolly. "If Robert Fenmore can tell us more of the events of last night than anyone else we must thoroughly scrutinise everything which touches him."

For a moment Marion Paul looked as though she would make a strong objection to Blake's arbitrary action, but evidently she thought better of it, for she bit her lip and said nothing. Closing the writing-case with a snap she rose and bowed coldly.

"I hope your investigations will tell you something of value," she said.

Then she was gone, and as the front door slammed behind her the inspector turned to Blake.

"She was huffy with you," he said. "Why did you want to keep the letter?"

"I took that method of angering her," replied Blake. "I wanted to get rid of her, and knew if I upset her temper she would leave. Marion Paul is too clever to argue when she is out of temper."

"But what should she argue about?" asked the inspector, in surprise.

"Perhaps the letter," rejoined Blake vaguely. And with that, he started for the kitchen. There was little of interest there beyond the window by which the intruder had come. A cursory examination of this showed that the catch had been forced back with a thin-bladed knife of some sort.

After going over it with the aid of the pocket glass Blake raised the sash and climbed over the sill, letting himself down to the roof of the outbuilding, which butted up against the wall of the house. Making his way cautiously down the sloping surface he paused at the edge, and, gauging the distance to the ground, made the jump. He landed lightly, and set himself to examine the footprints, which could be seen leading to the fence at the rear. Owing to the dry condition of the ground, they were not very distinct, but by lying flat on the ground he could make out the shape and size fairly well.

First he drew out a small pocket measure marked in millimetres and centimetres. With this he went over the print he was examining, taking the length of it and the breadth of the sole and heel. Then he went on to the next, and did likewise, jotting down the results in a notebook.

From the second print he went on to the fence and took the measurements of one of those there, and with that he rose. It was not so easy getting back to the roof of the outbuilding as it was to descend, but Blake managed it without assistance, at the same time proving that an active individual could have gained access to the flat that way.

He returned with the inspector to the sitting-room, and on their arrival there they found that the man had arrived from Scotland Yard with the photographic proofs of the fingerprints which had been found on the safe. The inspector had also taken the precaution to take prints of the fingers of both Marion Paul and the maid, and these, too, had been photographed.

They went to work at once to compare them and endeavour to discover if there were any amongst them which did not belong to either the mistress or the maid, but at the end of half an hour's hard work they were forced to give it up. In all of them there was none which did not correspond with the copies taken. Therefore, it was obvious that whoever had broken into the safe the previous night had not only been an expert safe-breaker but had also been clever enough to wear gloves of some sort.

When he was quite convinced that this was the case Blake rose and made to depart.

"I am going to Baker Street now, inspector," he said. "I want to give this thing some considerable thought, but just as soon as I arrive at an independent theory of some description I will make a move in the matter."

"Then that means that you will take on the case?" asked Inspector Thomas quickly.

Blake nodded.

"Oh, yes! I don't mind saying that it presents some points of great interest. By the way, I think you said it was your intention to find Robert Fenmore, if possible?"

"I have two men on that job already. I am inclined to think that Miss Paul has given us a strong clue."

"Perhaps," rejoined Blake. "At any rate, it can do no harm to discover his whereabouts, if possible. I myself propose to do so."

Beyond that Blake would say nothing, and a few moments later took his leave. Hailing a taxi he drove straight to Baker Street. Tinker had gone to the City early in the morning on a matter connected with some business Blake was doing for the Government, and had not yet returned. So casting aside his hat and coat Blake filled a pipe and drew up the big easy-chair in front of the fire.

From outside came the roar of the city as London went about its business. From the very beginning of the war the cool sanity of the great city had been a marvellous thing, and now that Christmas was close at hand, it was proving that though the burden of the nation was great, and suffering and sorrow had entered many homes, it would still present a smiling front to the world and make it Christmas as usual as far as possible.

Though the event was still some ten days away, the streets were filled with bustling crowds, and even in the Baker Street apartments there were many signs that Christmas was near, for already there had arrived cards and packages from far distant corners of the earth.

Blake's face looked rather grim as his gaze fell upon some which had arrived by the last post. It was one of the ironies of his profession that he should sit in the midst of such tokens of peace and goodwill while men shed their blood in savage warfare so near at hand, and that through it all he should be applying his mind to the solution of the taking of another life, not in the more gigantic warfare of nations but by secret murder.

He shook the oppressive thought from him and set himself to marshal the points he had noted during his examination of the flat, first enclosing the whole thing within the imaginary circle which he invariably drew about every case. First he took the flat itself, considering it in the same sequence as he had examined it, that is the sitting-room first.

"It is a strange thing," he muttered, "that a struggle, violent enough to upset the room as it was upset, should do so little real damage. Five pounds would cover the lot. It might not be so strange if that peculiarity was attached to but one part of the room which might have escaped, but that it should apply to the whole room is—peculiar. Every section of the apartment suffered, and in every single instance only the cheapest ornaments were broken. Point number one.

"Now another strange thing is that a large vase of thin glass, and filled with water, should fall a considerable distance to the floor and not break. Point two.

"Following that, the flowers which it contained were for some reason immediately removed by the maid and burned. Point three. Query: Why were they not thrown in the dust along with other rubbish, for there was some in the box showing that it had not been burned along with the flowers.

"Now to come to the missing necklace. I must confess that there is a good deal of mystery attached to that. If the one who murdered Craig also stole the necklace, and his— or her— visit to the flat was with that purpose, then the suggestions which Marion Paul makes are certainly not to be ignored. But against that comes the personality of the man upon whom she throws suspicion.

"Of course, every man with red blood in him is capable of killing under certain circumstances, whether it be in defence of his country or his own honour. But it is only a very small percentage of mankind which can deliberately plan a murder and carry it out. *And that is what the murder of Harold Craig was.* It was a carefully-planned murder, and carried out with no little ability, but it will be different from all other murders if there is not one flaw in it.

"The main point at the moment is to discover exactly what connection the Fenmore necklace has with the murder. Why was it sent to Mrs. Fenmore, and who sent it? Was it the murderer? If so, who could have an interest in the matter sufficiently great to steal the necklace, and when discovered by Craig to commit murder?

"On the face of it it points very strongly to Fenmore himself. One can theorise and imagine him wandering about under a changed name, realising the enormity of his past madness. Then one can see him driven desperate by remorse, and in his madness vowing to repair, as far as possible, the damage he has done.

"He makes up his mind to steal the necklace from the woman to whom he gave it, and to return it to his wife. He watches Marion Paul, and discovers the night on which she was at the theatre without the necklace. Then he goes to the flat, breaks in, gets what he is after, but, before making his escape, is surprised by his cousin, Craig, whom he finds has become very attentive to Marion Paul.

"A struggle ensues, and Craig is killed. But there that theory breaks down, for the simple reason that the murder was planned.

"But if Fenmore did not commit the crime, who had interest

enough to plan it and send the necklace back to his wife? It might be suggested that Mrs. Fenmore might have done so, but from what I know of that little lady I think she can be eliminated from the matter without hesitation. And that brings me to the point where I might make a more detailed examination of the letter which Bob Fenmore sent to Marion Paul with the necklace."

As he muttered the thought Blake thrust his hand in his pocket and took out the note. Spreading it out he read it over very carefully. When he had finished he folded it up very thoughtfully, and for a long time sat perfectly motionless. At last he stirred.

"It is the most peculiar letter I have ever read in my life," he muttered. "If Bob Fenmore sent that letter to Marion Paul on the day he disappeared, if he were callous enough to address her in that fashion on the very day he was leaving home, because he had brought ruin and unhappiness upon it, then he is even worse than gossip says, and easily capable of both theft and murder.

"No matter how bad a man had been he would scarcely send his last possession to an actress and leave his own wife stranded. And yet that is exactly what this letter seems to say Bob Fenmore did. Marion Paul, Marion— Good heavens, why didn't that occur to me before! Their names are exactly the same. Let me read the letter again."

Quickly he unfolded it, and once more scanned the words. Then he looked up, and, as he did so, a cold glint came into his eyes.

"I believe—I really believe that this letter was never intended for Marion Paul, and that means the necklace was never intended for her, either. It is more the letter of a desperate man to his wife when he sees all too late where his folly has brought him. That phrase about his realisation of his love for her was meant for his wife. He would never have written that to Marion Paul.

"Then, if that theory is correct, how did Marion Paul come into possession of the letter and necklace? That is certainly a point which must be cleared up. A great deal hangs on it. Now I wonder if Mrs. Fenmore has ever seen this letter. It would seem not. But if Fenmore wrote it, and intended it for her, why did it never reach her? That at once brings in the possibility of another individual—someone to whose interest it was that the letter should never reach Marion Fenmore, and that her husband should be discredited completely in her eyes.

"There could be no surer way of accomplishing that than by the way which was taken. And now to go back to the scene of the murder. If the footprints at the rear were made by the murderer, it is difficult for me to understand why there was such a struggle, for those footprints were made by a small individual—one who must have been a great deal smaller and less muscular than the dead man. Their measurements prove that point. But the cardinal fact is this: The crime which was committed was premeditated. The perpetrator was not only aware that Marion Paul was not wearing it that night, but also knew that Craig would be coming alone to the flat. I will stake my professional reputation on that."

Unconsciously Blake had thrust his hand in his pocket, and now he drew out the object which he had discovered in the folds of the table-cover back in the sitting-room of Marion Paul's flat. He stared at it for a moment uncomprehendingly, then suddenly it flashed upon him where he had found it, and he bent forward to examine it more closely. It was the single petal of a red rose which must have fallen from the bloom when the vase was lifted back on to the table.

Beneath the light he could see that there were one or two peculiar bluish spots on it, and when he was close to it, he noticed that it had a peculiar odour. He rose and walked to the desk where the light was stronger, and there discovered that there were many smaller spots which he had not noticed before. The odour was so distinct and unlike that of the rose that it puzzled him, and he concluded that it must come from the spots which he could see.

Holding it carefully, he started for the laboratory, in order to apply a chemical test to the spots, and had reached the passage which ran past Tinker's room, when suddenly everything about him seemed to heave upwards, then was blotted out completely, and he collapsed in a heap on the floor.

The Second Chapter.   Letters from Home—Bob Fenmore's Heroism.

AT the front. What a world of meaning that simple phrase carries to the man who has lain in the trenches night after night and day after day, while the great missiles of death and destruction whine and whistle and moan their way overhead. Miles and miles of hastily made trenches, which the rain and hail and sleet have turned into icy sewers of peril. Sodden ground from which the water oozes like the drops from a sponge— sticky, greasy mud, which clings to one like great lumps of glue— smoking horizon and bleeding earth with the awful staging of war, and the setting of wounded men and beasts with the ever present menace of the sudden attack.

No sun— nothing but the grey pall of winter, and the steady downpour which had held for days. And still man and beast must go through it, and keep their eyes always to the front, until earth and tree and sky seemed to grow crimson with the unchanging grimness of it all.

On the left wing of the British, where the flower of the German troops were being hurled with almost superhuman savagery, these conditions had prevailed for days. There, where the Fusiliers had day after day, sleeping on the sodden ground, and standing to the waist in icy water, the only consolation had been that the enemy must do it too.

To the rear of the British the artillery kept up a continual bombardment of the German position, while from the high ground in front the guns of the enemy replied defiantly. From each side the sorties had been made daily—sometimes many in a day; but so far, no appreciable progress had been made by either side.

The main body of the Germans was strongly entrenched about the small village in front, from which the terrified inhabitants had fled long since. To capture that position was an essential part of the British plan, and to hold it a thing which the enemy must do at all costs. It was the key to a larger and more important position, and only when the British had taken it could the main body behind push through the gap.

Never before had that tiny village loomed with such importance in the plans of men and nations, and probably it never would again. Nor could it wish to. Its glory had come on the wind of destruction, and now it lay ruined, deserted and forlorn—the empty husk of what had once been that which goes to make up the community of men—the place of their birth, the centre of their sorrows and their joys.

But though Nature and man had combined to create chaos and though the boys in the trenches were soaking wet and almost worn out, there was still sufficient spirit left in the —th Fusiliers for eyes to light up, and the landscape to grow strangely blurred on the day letters arrived from home. Home— what the word meant to those lads in the trenches who had been hurled from green and peaceful Britain into a roaring holocaust of bleeding death, knowing not where they were, or what might be the conditions beyond where they could not see.

Water and slush and cold, and even the whining shells overhead were forgotten, as they read of things at home. There sat a grizzled sergeant on the lip of the trench, reading many closely written pages, telling of how the folks were getting on in his absence, and waiting for him to come home. Jimmie, the eldest boy had found a good job, and was bringing in his few shillings a week, with all the importance of the grown man. Annie was a good girl, and was helping mother nobly. The baby had cut another tooth, and Annie had taught it to say "dada" against the time when "dada" would come home. And the wife was well, and watching and praying for her man.

A little farther down the trench was a youngster of scarcely nineteen, whose eyes grew blurred as he read the crabbed hand of the old mother back in Lincolnshire. He was her only boy, but she had given him freely to the service of her country; but oh, what a heartache there was behind those words which tried to be so brave.

And on again was a fine specimen of young manhood devouring the thick budget from the girl he had left back home—dwelling over and over on the little tender passages of love, which were meant for his eyes, and his alone.

Letters from mother, and wife, and sweetheart; from sister, and brother, and proud father—from the children, too, even to the first sprawling sentences of the youngest, they were all represented.

Eyes grew misty, chests heaved tumultuously, and fingers shook, as no onslaught of the enemy had ever made them shake, as the boys in the trenches read them and re-read them.

From one end of the trench to the other the sheets fluttered in the hands of the eager readers. All had some cheering message to make him happy, and spur him on to braver deeds, than ever. All? No, not all. Half-way down the trench sitting alone, and staring gloomily before him was a man for whom there had been nothing. The white line showed on the back of his hand with the strength of his clenched fist, and a tiny trickle of blood was beginning to flow from his lip, as unconsciously he bit it in the agony of his suffering.

Private Robert Fraser of the —th Fusiliers was a taciturn and unapproachable member of that body; but if his mates did not make free with him, they had a large respect for his ability as a soldier. When there was any fighting to do, Private Fraser was always to be found in the front ranks, and when the trenches of the enemy were rushed at the point of the bayonet, Private Fraser was there fighting with terrible ferocity.

He had joined in London on the outbreak of war, and from the very first the keen eyes of the sergeant had seen that he was an experienced soldier. The usual question as to whether he had served before was met by the reply that he had—in South Africa. But there the information ended, and Private Fraser's sergeant never dreamed that one valued member of his company was a man who, as Lieutenant Robert Fenmore had received special mention in South Africa for gallant conduct under fire. And Private Fraser alone of all the company had received no letter from home.

As he watched the faces of his companions, a bitter flood engulfed his soul, and he almost cried aloud in his suffering. No one but Bob Fenmore knew what he had gone through since that morning, when, after writing a farewell note to his wife, he had gone forth from his home, bidding it farewell forever.

Once away from all the old life which had dragged him down and down like a relentless octopus, and living the clean hard-bitten life of the regiment, he had got a new focus of himself and the picture he had seen had sickened him to the soul. He saw himself clothed in all the mad folly of the gambler, and he saw, in all its naked truth, the treatment he had handed out to his wife.

And as each day dragged out its torturing course, and the long nights of sleepless agony came, he fought out his fight, but never did he win. More and more there came to him the picture of his wife. His mind would conquer his sternest resolve, and leap back to the happy days of the honeymoon, when he had possessed all her love, and when she had been as a happy child, just realising the joys of existing.

As the shells screamed past, and the bullets zipped viciously, her face would rise up before him. and her soft eyes would look at him appealingly, as she had looked when the demon of chance again claimed him. But that was all gone now. He had sacrificed happiness to folly, and for the rest of his life must drag out a tortured existence, knowing that he loved her beyond all, but knowing it too late.

And that was why Private Fraser was always in the thick of the fight. In death only could he find release, and death he sought every waking hour.

Not for long were the boys of the —th Fusiliers allowed to read of home in peace. Far up the line a sharp command rang out, just as the fire from the artillery of the enemy grew more violent than ever.

Another charge was to be made upon the trenches of the Germans, and as a second command came, every man leaped for his rifle. Then such a roaring chaos broke loose that it was difficult even to think coherently.

All along the line the khaki-clad figures leaped up, and, with bayonets fixed, scrambled over the lip of the trench, and with a hoarse cheer plunged through the stretch of mud and slush towards the trenches of the Germans.

A withering fire met them, but though men fell on every side they kept on unwaveringly, confident of the result, if once they could bring the issue down to cold steel.

Side by side with the sergeant Private Fraser dashed forward, all the agony of the past half hour concentrated in one mad determination to get to grips, and ease his suffering by violent physical combat. A wild look was in his eyes, and unconsciously he was cursing aloud, as strong men will in times of great stress.

The sergeant looked at him curiously as they raced onward together, then came the crash of steel on steel, and for a time he saw him no more. But many there were who did see him, and marvel at the almost unbelievable strength of his attack.

Man after man of the enemy went down before him, and still he remained unscathed. Those who knew him not might have thought he was favoured of the gods, but in his heart he knew that he remained unscathed only because he had not yet suffered enough.

It was utterly impossible for human beings to withstand such an attack as the —th Fusiliers delivered. Slowly but surely the enemy gave way, until they had been forced back to the shelter of a second line of trenches.

Then suddenly it was seen that large reinforcements were coming to their assistance, and the retreat was sounded. Then the reinforcements of the enemy swept up, and a terrific fusillade was poured in upon the British. They retreated, that was all they could do; but not even that withering fire from the enemy could force them back to the trench where they had been when the letters from home arrived.

They dropped back into the first trench they had captured, and nothing would budge them.

It was when they had arrived there, and were replying to the fire of the enemy, that the word went down the line that the sergeant was missing. Where was he? Then someone remembered that he had fallen during the retreat, and just as that information passed along every man gasped, as a tall figure leaped from the trench and dashed ahead in the very teeth of the leaden hail which was sweeping across the open. It was Private Robert Fraser.

Unconsciously he had adopted a zig-zag motion, and as he drew ever nearer to the break of ground where the retreat had been sounded, his comrades held their breath, suffering physically with the strain of the thing.

Once he staggered and dropped to his knees, but in a moment he was up again and going forward. Then he dipped over the ridge of ground and disappeared.

A minute passed, two minutes, then the eager watchers saw him reappear, staggering towards them with a burden on his back. A great cheer went up from them, but it was quickly changed to a gasp of anxiety, as once more he went to his knees. But he struggled up gamely, and ever so slowly recommenced his progress.

Foot by foot he came on, nearer and nearer he got to the British trench, though not a man in it thought he would ever make it. The flying bullets were too thick for a man to survive them for long. But against all the laws of chance, he was able to stagger on until his comrades could see that he was blinded from the stream of blood which was pouring from a wound in the head.

Great patches of crimson were on his coat and trousers too, and it was plain that he had been wounded several times. Then they saw that the man on his back was the sergeant, and his lips could be seen moving. Those who knew him knew that he was urging his bearer to leave him and reach the trench before he was hit again; but evidently Private Fraser was deaf to all, and obsessed by only one idea—to make the trench with his sergeant, cost what it might.

He was drawing very near now, and as his comrades saw the look of agonised determination on his face, half-a-dozen of them leaped up, and rushing forward, dragged rescuer and rescued to shelter.

Then the man who had just done the deed of a hero collapsed in a heap in the water-filled trench, and was frankly sick.

Willing hands there were to lift him up, and soon the brave lads of the Red Cross took him in charge and carried him to the rear. In time the doctor came to him, but when he saw the condition he was in his head shook gravely. One bullet had ploughed a deep furrow along his scalp, another had gone through his left lung, a third had caught him in the hip, and still a fourth had struck him on the right leg just below the knee.

It was the one which had passed through his lung that caused the doctor to shake his head, but nevertheless he went to work and did his best for him. Then other bearers took him up, and carried him back to a village still farther to the rear, where he was put to bed in a tiny cottage.

But of all this Private Robert Fraser had no consciousness, for he was raving and babbling with an insane savagery which, experienced though she was, caused the Red Cross nurse to pale. But back in the firing line a keen-eyed commander had seen what had happened, and while he lay the prey of feverish insanity, the name of Private Fraser was being ascertained in order that he should be recommended for the greatest prize a soldier can win—the plain little cross bearing the words "For Valour"—Britain's Victoria Cross.

IT is a far cry from the trenches in France and Belgium to the complications of a murder investigation in London, but Fate in her vagaries recks not of places or distances, and it was one of her fancies that the moment when Bob Fenmore, alias Private Fraser, should so gallantly rescue his sergeant in the face of a murderous fire, should be the same one which saw the crashing to the floor of Sexton Blake while on his way to the laboratory to examine the rose-petal which he had found in the sitting-room of Marion Paul's flat.

And the fickle dame also chose that, about ten minutes after he had been lying there unconscious, Tinker and Pedro should reach home on their return from the City. On seeing his master's hat and coat in the consulting-room, Tinker knew that Blake must be at home, so immediately on entering he called.

On receiving no answer he at once concluded that Blake had passed through to the laboratory, so throwing open the door leading to the passage he started down it. Half way down he saw Blake lying in a heap just outside his bed-room.

With a startled exclamation of alarm, he ran forward and bent over his master. As he saw Blake's face, his eyes widened with fear, for the features were swollen and almost black. Grasping Blake beneath the shoulders, he dragged him back along the hall towards the consulting-room, and laying him on the couch rang for Mrs. Bardell. When she arrived he cut short her startled cry and jerked:

"Something has happened to the guv'nor! Get hot water, quick! Be sure it is boiling."

Then, as she hurried away, he leaped for the 'phone and rang up Dr. Henderson, Blake's own physician, who lived in the next street.

Luckily, he caught the doctor at home, and impressing upon him the need for urgency slammed up the receiver and hurried back to Blake. There was no change in his condition. His face was still swollen and black, and his pulse was scarcely perceptible.

In a fever of fear Tinker gazed about him wildly for some means of reviving his master, whom he could see was in a very critical condition and apparently growing rapidly worse. His eyes lit on a small medicine-case which stood in the corner, and hastening towards it he took out a small vial of strychnine and a hypodermic syringe. Gathering a tiny bit of the powerful drug into the syringe he hurried back to the couch and, baring Blake's arm, made an injection. Then he waited anxiously with his fingers on Blake's pulse.

For a time it showed no change, then ever so slowly it grew stronger until it became quite distinct. But as yet Blake showed no signs of consciousness, nor did the swollen condition of his features relax.

At this moment Mrs. Bardell rushed in, carrying a large jug of boiling water, and simultaneously Dr. Henderson arrived. He hurried forward with a word of alarm as he saw Blake's condition, and gazed down gravely at him.

"What has happened, Tinker?" he asked sharply.

"I don't know, doctor," answered the lad. "I got home a few moments ago, and not seeing the guv'nor in here went through to the laboratory to look for him. I found him lying on the floor just outside my bed-room door in this condition. I dragged him in here, and rang you up at once."

"Have you done anything yourself?"

"Yes, sir. His pulse was so weak I was frightened, and gave him a small injection of strychnine."

"How much?" asked the doctor sharply.

"About a sixtieth of a grain."

"Ah, that was safe, and I don't know but what you did the best thing. Is that water boiling?"

"Yes, sir. Mrs. Bardell just brought it in."

"Very well, get me a couple of towels. I can't imagine what has happened to Blake. At first I thought it was apoplexy, but it isn't. His eyes look queer beneath the lids. The only thing to do is to try to get him conscious and ask him what happened. Then we will know what to do for him."

Tinker hastened away to get the towels, and in a moment returned with them. In the meantime the doctor had poured some strong stimulant down Blake's throat, and now dipping the towels in the boiling water he signed to Tinker to open Blake's shirt at the throat. Then he applied the hot towels to the region over the heart, and held it there.

Tinker vigorously massaged his master's wrists.

For a few moments there was no perceptible change, but at the end of that time the terrible black look left the face, and a little later Blake's lids flickered. A further bit of treatment caused them to open, and he looked up at them.

"What is it?" asked the doctor, bending forward quickly. "What has happened to you? Tell me, if you understand. Then I shall know what to do."

"Poison," murmured Blake weakly, then again relapsed. Like a flash the doctor grasped him under the arms, and said jerkingly to Tinker:

"Up with him, my lad! His only chance lies in our keeping him from sinking back into a state of coma. We must walk him up and down until he has conquered it."

Tinker leaped to his assistance, and taking him one on either side they began walking him up and down the room, working his arms and beating his body as they did so.

Up and down, up and down, up and down they went, and for a long time Blake hung a dead weight on their arms, but at last the awful limpness seemed to leave him a little, and they could see that though he was only half conscious he realised what they were doing, and was making an effort to help them.

Still they kept it up, not relaxing for a single moment, and at the end of an hour they had the satisfaction of seeing their efforts rewarded.

Blake's eyes opened, and this time he did not sink back into unconsciousness. His legs, too, became controlled by his will, and at the end of another twenty minutes he was almost able to manage by himself, and they saw that they had conquered. But not for another hour did they desist, and then all three, thoroughly exhausted by the shock, seated themselves. The doctor prepared another dose for Blake and forced him to drink it. Then, when some colour had returned to the latter's features, he said:

"Now then, Blake, what happened? I have seen you ill at different times, but you never gave me a greater scare than you did to-day. In fact, if it hadn't been that Tinker did exactly the right thing, I don't know that I could have saved you. You said you were poisoned. How did it occur?"

Blake smiled wanly.

"I was going to the laboratory to make an examination of a specimen," he said. "I was careless with it, and it caught me as you have seen. That is all."

"Well, you take my advice and be more careful in future,"

rejoined the doctor. "Good men are scarce, and we are losing enough in the trenches without you poisoning yourself here."

After a little more of this sort of thing—for he was very fond of Blake, he took his departure. No sooner had the door closed behind him than Blake turned to Tinker.

"Thank you, my lad, for your prompt measures," he said quietly. "It only adds to the great debt I already owe you, and I think you know how I feel about it."

"Oh, I didn't do anything," mumbled Tinker. Then, irrelevantly: "You scared the life nearly out of me."

"I am sorry my lad. By the way, when I was overcome, I was carrying the petal of a rose in my hand. Did you see it when you found me?"

"Why, it seems to me I did see something fall from your hand, guv'nor. Was it red?"

"Yes."

"Then I am certain I saw it. It must be lying on the floor in the passage. I will go and see."

"Do, please, my lad. But don't hold it near your face; it is dangerous."

"Good heavens, guv'nor, was that what poisoned you?"

"I strongly suspect so Tinker, although I am not yet certain. However, don't run any risks."

"All right, sir, I'll be careful," responded the lad, as he rose and left the room. He returned a few moments later, holding at arm's length between his fingers the petal of a red rose. Blake nodded as he saw it.

"That is it, my lad. Just lay it on the desk for the present."

Tinker did as he was ordered, and turned back to his master.

"What does it mean, guv'nor?" he asked.

Blake smiled.

"It has some connection with the murder which took place last night, my lad."

"Do you mean the murder of the man Craig, sir?"

"Yes."

"Then you are on the case, guv'nor?"

Again Blake nodded.

"I am, my lad, and before many minutes have gone you are going to be on it, too. Sit down, Tinker, I wish to speak to you."

The lad seated himself in a chair, and gave Blake his attention.

"Inspector Thomas called here this morning after you had gone to the City, my lad, and asked me to assist him in rounding up the individual who had committed the murder. I had just finished reading the newspaper reports, so was already in possession of some of the facts. But Inspector Thomas had some information on the subject which had been withheld from the Press, and some of it seemed to point definitely to a possible culprit. At least, that is the opinion of the inspector."

"And that means it isn't yours," grinned Tinker.

"Perhaps," said Blake. "That remains to be seen. As a matter of fact, I haven't formed any definite theory yet, though one or two are beginning to form in my mind. The rose petal which you just laid on the desk will yet prove to have a strong connection with the case, or I shall be very much mistaken. But so far the inspector has no inkling that I think so. In fact, he suspects nothing regarding it, and at present I think the information is best kept to ourselves. Briefly, my lad, there was a large vase of roses on the table in the room where the murder took place. They were destroyed by the maid, but she overlooked this petal which had fallen to the floor and had become concealed in the folds of the table-cover. I noticed it in my examination of the room, and put it in my pocket. But it was not until I had been home some little time that it occurred to me to examine it. Then it was that I noticed the little bluish spots on it, and since the unexplained way in which the roses had been destroyed had already roused my curiosity, I determined to take the petal to the laboratory and make a chemical examination of the spots.

"I had been bending closely over it there, and it was immediately after that that I was overcome. There is no doubt in my mind but that those bluish spots were caused by a powerful poison being sprayed on the flowers, and if that is so then we haven't far to look for the cause of Craig's death. I shall prove that point later on.

"Now, as you will have gathered from the papers, the general impression is that Craig met his death through poison, but how it was administered no one seems to know. At first it was thought that he had died in an epileptic fit, but the disordered condition of the room indicated that a severe struggle had taken place, and when a medical examination had been made it was decided that he had been poisoned, though I believe the nature of the drug has not yet been ascertained.

"But when I made an examination of the room I was struck by one or two things of a peculiar nature, and I have come to the conclusion that the murder of Craig was premeditated, and that the disorder of the room was not caused by a struggle, but that it had been deliberately arranged to look as though one had taken place. It is my opinion that we shall eventually find that this affair was most carefully planned and executed. Therefore, we must search for any flaws, and in lighting on this rose petal, which by accident we are led to suspect is poisoned, we may have found the thread which will eventually lead us to a solution of the mystery.

"I have gone into this at some length, Tinker, because I want you to know my point of view in the matter. Do not imagine that I suspect any particular person. I don't—yet. But there are a few things to be explained, and that explanation we must have. The papers do not yet know, and therefore you do not know, that there was also a robbery there last night. Only one thing was taken, and that was the famous Fenmore necklace of which you read some three or four months ago when London was talking of the disappearance of Robert Fenmore.

"That same theft, plus something which Marion Paul told the inspector, leads him to think that he has struck a correct solution of the affair. But he has formed his theory without knowing of the poisoned flowers, and without suspecting that the condition of the room was not due to a struggle. For that reason I do not want you to go ahead with either his theory in your mind or even mine. I want your mind to be perfectly free to register every impression it receives in order that you may report to me without any bias.

"The points which I wish to investigate more particularly have their genesis at the flat where the murder was committed. Therefore you will go there and start to work. Now the flat is situated in the — Hotel, a small private hotel in Knightsbridge. You will have read in the papers how it was thought the murderer had gained access to the flat by way of some outbuildings at the rear. That may or may not be so, but one thing is certain—someone entered the flat by that way last evening.

"I want you to go there and hang about. Keep your eyes open to see if Marion Paul puts in an appearance. If so, follow her wherever she goes. She spent last night and is staying to-day at a hotel in the neighbourhood, but the inspector said she would probably return to the flat this afternoon. Stay there until to-night, and when it is dark go round to the rear. If you can manage to get into the flat, so much the better. In case you should succeed in doing so, I will give you a rough plan of the place, showing the different rooms.

"On it you will see the location of the guest-room, which I imagine would be the best for purposes of concealment if you managed an entry. When you furnish me a report of your investigations there, I may be able to decide whether the murder was an inside job or an outside one. On that point I am still undecided. Now, are you quite clear in your mind as to what you have to do?"

"Quite, guv'nor. I shall go round there at once, and keep my eyes peeled. Are you sure you are feeling well enough for me to leave?"

"Oh, I shall be all right now, my lad. I am feeling much better. By the way, you said my face was swollen when I was unconscious. Was there anything else in my condition which attracted your attention?"

"Only that it was black, guv'nor. It did give me a scare."

"Black, eh? That was exactly the condition of the murdered man, too. I think there is no question but that the roses were the cause of his death, but the question is: Who sprayed them with the poison? Before you go, Tinker, just hand me volume 'P' of the 'Information Index.' Thank you."

As Tinker took his cap and started out, Blake opened the volume the lad had given him until he came to a page which was headed "Marion Paul." The "Information Index" at Baker Street was the result of any bits of information gathered by both Blake and Tinker regarding any person in the public eye, and in common with others, several facts had been gathered and annotated regarding Marion Paul, the famous music-hall star. Blake read over the page slowly:

"Paul, Marion—music-hall artiste. Born in Spain, and educated at a Madrid dancing school. Went to Russia at the age of sixteen, and attended a ballet school. Made her first appearance in Vienna at the age of twenty, where she was received favourably. Her beauty was an undoubted asset to her stage career, and in Vienna she had many offers of marriage. It is not generally known that while there she was secretly married to Professor Johann Mulberg, a research chemist of dubious antecedents. From Vienna she went to Berlin, where, it is said, she was the cause of more than one duel. While there one of her lovers, a youth of noble family, was mysteriously killed, and rumour had it that another had committed the crime through jealousy, though no one was brought to book for the deed. Shortly after that she left Berlin, going to Paris, and then to Madrid. From the latter place she came to London, where she still remains. The whereabouts of her husband are unknown. It has been said that he died in Berlin. Whether that be so or not, he has not appeared in London, and since scarcely anyone knows of the marriage, he has been practically forgotten."

That was the report, and before laying down the book, Blake read it over twice. Then he rose, and moving weakly towards the desk, reached for a pad of telegraph forms. Seating himself at the desk, he began to write. The first form he addressed in code to an agent of his in New York, and, decoded, it read as follows:

"When you were in Berlin at the time of Marion Paul's presence there, did you see anything of her supposed husband? If so, do you know what became of him? Cable at once all you can tell me of the matter."

Tearing this off, he filled in a second one. This was addressed to another agent in Madrid, and ran thus:

"Wire me all you know of Marion Paul, born Madrid twenty-seven years ago. Look up record, and also endeavour to trace whereabouts of Professor Johann Mulberg, whom she is supposed to have married secretly in Vienna seven years ago. You will probably get track of him in Berlin or Vienna, places where, owing to war, I can't make investigations.   B."

Then he rang for Mrs. Bardell, and giving the two messages to her, told her to send for a messenger-boy and get them away at once. Scarcely had he done so when the street doorbell rang, and a few moments later Mrs. Bardell ushered in a lady. Blake glanced up inquiringly as he heard the swish of skirts; then, as he recognised who it was, he smiled in welcome. It was Mademoiselle Yvonne.

"It is a pleasure to see you," he said, as he shook hands. "I thought you were away on the yacht, doing something for the Admiralty."

She smiled up into his eyes, then her face grew grave.

"You look ill. What is the matter?"

"Oh, nothing much, I assure you," he replied. "I had a little accident this morning, and was overcome for a time. Thanks to Tinker and Dr. Henderson, I am feeling much better now. I shall be all right by to-morrow. But about yourself. What brings you to town? Have you come up to prepare for Christmas?"

She sank into the big easy-chair in front of the fire, and shook her head.

"No. I was called here by an urgent telegram from a friend of mine. I got in last evening, and have been with her almost ever since. It is something connected with her that has brought me to see you. I know you are frightfully busy, but I want you to help me."

Blake laughed.

"Then you are here as a client?"

"Yes."

"In that case, I must do all I can to help you. It will be the first time I have had the pleasure of receiving you as such."

"You needn't be amused. I assure you it is a serious matter. I am dreadfully upset about it."

"Ah, forgive me. Tell me what is the trouble."

"Do you remember the disappearance of Bob Fenmore about four months ago?"

"What—another?" murmured Blake.

"Another!" she echoed sharply. "What do you mean by that?"

"I may tell you later. Go on, please."

"Well, I had a good deal to do with that disappearance."

It was Blake's turn to be surprised.

"You?" he said. "In what way?"

"Listen, and I will tell you. Only let me say now that what I did I did for what I thought was his own good. Unfortunately, I left London the same day myself, and so did not know until yesterday what had really taken place. I first took a hand in the matter when I heard what a fool he was making of himself over gambling.

"Marion Fenmore is a dear friend of mine, and for her sake I resolved to teach him a lesson. Well, to make a long story short, I found out where he was doing his gaming, and went there to watch him. The first night I was there I saw that the game was crooked, and that he could not win in any case. He was with Marion Paul, and it did not take me long to discover that she was nothing but a highly-paid tout for the place. But I did not discover until later that she and the man who was dealing the game—it was faro—had combined to ruin Bob Fenmore.

"It was the man's idea, and she was his tool—well paid, beyond doubt. On the morning after the game I took the pains to follow the man who had done the dealing, for I had become convinced that he was disguised. My suspicions proved correct, for I was able to follow him home, and before I left him I had discovered his identity. The next night I went to the gaming place early—it was the old Frileti's in Wilton Crescent—and sought an interview with the man I had followed. He gave me one reluctantly, and there and then I demanded that he sell me the place. He laughed at me, but when I told him that I had seen his crooked play, and that I would inform the police regarding the place, he climbed down, and offered me a partnership.

"Well, we compromised on that, and I put up ten thousand pounds as a half share, stipulating that I should do all the dealing in the private room. He objected again, but I dominated him from the start, and eventually he gave in. That same night I took over the table, and I was not surprised to see Bob Fenmore turn up again in company with Marion Paul.

"Evidently my partner had informed her of the change, and had told her I was all right, for she showed no surprise when she saw me at the table. For a week I dealt there every night, and for a week Bob Fenmore came. I won from him night after night, because, like the man before me, I was dealing a crooked game. At last he was cleaned out, and I knew that my object was accomplished. When the others had gone that night I had another interview with my partner, and told him I intended to keep not half of this week's winnings, but the whole of them. We had a strenuous time, but when l told him I had discovered his identity, he wilted at once, though, hard as he tried, he never discovered mine. Well, I took all the winnings—that is, the money I had won from Bob Fenmore and the other profits—and sent them to his wife, telling her that the money was really hers, and that it had been as much as stolen from her husband.

"I also warned her against the man who had posed as a faro dealer, and the same day left London. I have been so busy since that I have been unable to get up to town except on urgent business, and I really did not know how things had gone with Marion Fenmore.

"I received a wire yesterday, and came straight on from Dover. As I told you, I arrived early last evening, and went straight to see her. She was terribly ill, and quite out of her head. I listened to her ravings for some time, and discovered that something in particular was preying on her mind terribly.

"Poor little soul, she must have been suffering for weeks without a single individual to turn to for comfort. You know she is an orphan.

Well, as soon as I discovered what it was on her mind, I drove straight home and sent for my uncle. From him I found out what had been going on. He told me how Bob Fenmore had gone away, and had entirely disappeared, and how before he went he had sent to Marion Paul the famous Fenmore necklace with an affectionate letter. I was never more angry in my life. I thought I might succeed in teaching him a lesson, but it seems he is beyond help. A man that could do what he did is worthless, and Marion Fenmore is better without him. But she is crying for him, and now there is another reason why he must be found. That is why I have come to you. I want you to find Bob Fenmore."

"What is the other reason beside his wife's need of him?" asked Blake.

"I will tell you. He is now the father of a little son, and, ill as she is, his wife wants him back. She is so utterly proud of it, and cannot rest content until he is with her."

"Ah, I had no idea that was the case," said Blake gravely. "That little woman has suffered enough. I think it is time Bob Fenmore was found. By the way, before we discuss that phase of the matter further, I should like to ask you a question, if I may."

"Certainly. What is it?"

"Did you enter Marion Paul's apartment last night and take from the safe in the sitting-room the Fenmore necklace?"

A wave of crimson swept over Yvonne's face, suffusing her eyes.

"I—I—why, what do you mean?"

Blake smiled.

"You did, didn't you?"

The colour gradually receded from Yvonne's face, and presently she laughed outright.

"What if I say I did? Bob Fenmore had no right to give that necklace to Marion Paul."

"Are you quite sure he did?"

"Why, yes! All the world knows he did."

"Do you know, Yvonne, that the police are very anxious to find the person who entered Marion Paul's flat last night?"

"I suppose she will make a lot of publicity about the affair. But that doesn't worry me, and I don't think you will betray me. The necklace is Marion Fenmore's by right, and you know it."

"I am not questioning that. But do you mean to say you have not heard of any other reason why the police might wish to find the person who broke into the flat?"

Yvonne's eyes widened.

"No," she said quickly. "Is there another reason?"

"Have you not seen a paper to-day?"

"No. I was with Marion Fenmore all night, and to-day. I got away just before I came to see you, and haven't had a chance to see a paper. But I will confess that I made my way into Marion Paul's flat last night, and took the necklace from the safe. It was not difficult. I did it because when she was raving, Marion Fenmore revealed that her heart was breaking over her husband's callousness, and I determined that she should find the necklace beside her when she was better. But I know of no reason why the police should be anxious to find me."

"Then you are still unaware that there was a murder committed in the sitting-room of Marion Paul's flat last night, and that the general impression is that the person who stole the necklace and the murderer are one and the same."

"Good heavens! Are you in earnest?"

"Never more so in my life. I was called in on the case this morning. Inspector Thomas feels quite sure that when he finds the individual who took the necklace he will also have found the murderer."

"And you?"

"I? Oh, I think otherwise!"

"What makes the inspector think that?"

"I believe I am not betraying a confidence when I tell you that it is because of something Marion Paul told him. In fact, she casts a definite suspicion in a certain direction."

"Can you tell me upon whom?"

"You must understand that all this is quite in confidence, Yvonne. The person upon whom she casts suspicion is the same man whom you wish me to find—Bob Fenmore!"

"Oh, that is impossible, Mr. Blake. Whatever Bob Fenmore is he is not a murderer. But do you know the identity of the murdered man?"

"Yes. The man who was murdered was Fenmore's cousin, Harold Craig."

Yvonne gazed at him with wide eyes. Then she leaned forward.

"There is a great deal behind all this, Mr. Blake." she said quietly. "You know or suspect a great deal more than you have told me. Take me into your confidence, and let me help you in this. Nothing must reach Marion Fenmore. She is too delicate at present to stand any more suffering."

Blake nodded slowly.

"That is exactly what I intend to do, Yvonne. But before telling you anything further, I want to ask you a question."

"What is it?"

"What is the name of the man who posed as the faro dealer at Frileti's, and whom you suspected of being in league with Marion Paul to encompass Bob Fenmore's financial ruin?"

"What an extraordinary question," she gasped. "And what an odd thing that you should ask it now! The man was Harold Craig."

Again Blake nodded.

"Somehow I suspected that," he said quietly. "There is a whole lot regarding his connection with Marion Paul which needs explaining. Do you know of any reason, Yvonne, why he should have had an interest in Fenmore's ruin?"

"Well, the only thing I can suggest is revenge. He was very much in love with Marion Straight before she married Fenmore, and as soon as Fenmore started gambling again, he began going to the house very frequently. But you may rest assured nobody ever suspected that he was the proprietor of Frileti's. Whether he acquired it after Bob Fenmore began gambling again, I do not know, but he certainly used it for Fenmore's ruin."

"I see. Is the place closed now?"

"Yes. It was closed at the time of Fenmore's disappearance. I saw to that."

"There is one thing which you may be able to find out, Yvonne, and if you can it will be a great help to me."

"What is that?"

"When are you returning to the Fenmore place?"

"When I leave here."

"Good! I want you to find out from the servants all Fenmore's movements on the morning he disappeared. I know from what you have already told me that he was gaming at Frileti's, but I wish to know what he did afterwards. You should be able to find out from one of the servants."

"Bayles, his valet, is still there. He ought to know."

"Quite right. He should be the very one to tell you. I am keen to know, too, if there was anyone with Fenmore that morning—Craig, for instance."

"I shall do my best to find out. Do you mind telling me your reason?"

"Not at all. First, I shall tell you what I know about the murder, then you will understand much better."

Then Blake began, and related to Yvonne the details of the murder, which the papers had contained, going from that to the inspector's visit and his examination of the flat. After that he touched lightly on the theory the inspector had formed after hearing Marion Paul's story, and explained why there was a hue and cry after the missing Bob Fenmore. Then he dealt at length with his own observations, not forgetting the rose petal, and what had happened to him from a too close examination of it. Finally, he reached into his pocket, and drew out the note he had so coolly appropriated from Marion Paul.

"Just read that, Yvonne," he said; "then tell me what you think of it."

She took it from him wonderingly, and read what was written. She read it a second time, and still a third time before handing it back.

"It is a peculiar letter for a man like Bob Fenmore to write to a woman like Marion Paul," she said slowly. "When he realised that he had lost all his wife's money as well as his own it does not seem likely that he would send his last asset to the woman who had participated in his ruin. He must have realised her part in it. To my mind, it is much more the kind of letter he would have written to his wife before leaving when he realised what he had done. That one phrase where he says that all too late he realised that he loved her more than all, seems to indicate that my argument is sound. It is a phrase full of shame and regret and remorse. And he had no reason to write such a phrase to Marion Paul."

"And yet she seems to think that it was he who murdered Craig last night, and that one of his reasons was jealousy because Craig was so attentive to her," murmured Blake.

"Fiddlesticks!" snapped Yvonne. "The very thought of that woman makes me weary. What is her opinion worth? She also intimates that it was Fenmore who took the necklace from the safe, and he had nothing whatsoever to do with it."

"Tell me, Yvonne, what time was it last night when you were there?"

"I left Marion Fenmore's shortly after seven, and went straight to see my uncle. When I had found out from him what I wanted to know, I drove to the theatre where Marion Paul was on, and had a look at her. That was about half-past eight. I had no intention of attempting to get the necklace last night, but when I saw that she was not wearing it, I thought it was a pity not to follow the line Fate had given me. So I went at once to Knightsbridge, and reconnoitred. The result was that by way of the rear I got into the flat, and when I saw the safe in the sitting-room, I felt somehow that the necklace must be in it. That was about half-past nine, and there were no signs of Craig when I was there. The flat was quite deserted."

"He did not arrive until about ten," put in Blake. "But was the room in order when you were there?"

"No. I meant to speak of that before. It was upset dreadfully. It gave me a shock when I first entered, for I thought there must have been a scramble of some sort, and was afraid of running into someone. The whole room was askew."

"Did you notice if there was a vase of roses on the floor?"

"There was. I presume it was the same one of which you told me. And that reminds me of something. There was a distinct odour in the room, and I also noticed when I got out of the place that I was feeling slightly giddy. At the time I did not attach any importance to the feeling, but in the light of what you have told me, I am wondering if you are not right about the flowers having been sprayed with poison."

"At any rate, Yvonne, you have proved one of my theories. I mean the one that the room did not get into such a disordered condition owing to the struggle which is supposed to have taken place. It was carefully arranged to look like that. But whoever was responsible for it, unconsciously proved that they have a parsimonious element in their nature."

"How do you make that out?"

"Because the actual damage was so little. And that reluctance to sacrifice a few valuable ornaments for the greater deed will yet weave the cord by which we shall rope them in."

"Do you think Marion Paul might have had a hand in it?" asked Yvonne, after a slight pause.

"I wouldn't go so far as to say that. She may have a suspicion as to who did commit the crime, and I do not think she is sincere in intimating that Fenmore may have done it. When one analyses it, that theory does not become tenable. But it is too early yet for us to permit ourselves to make a definite theory. We must prove several points first, and to that we must gather a mass of information. That which you will discover at the Fenmore place will be an important item, and I shall be glad if you will tell me the result as soon as possible."

"You will hear from me some time to-night about that," she replied. "But what will you do about Bob Fenmore? Marion is suffering for him, and now that the baby has come she will not rest until she has him back. In her new-found joy she has forgiven all the past."

"For many reasons we must find him, if possible," rejoined Blake. "If the police find him first, he may find himself in a very awkward position, for with Marion Paul as a witness against him, anything we could say at present would avail him little. We might eventually clear him of the charge, but with the past behind him, I am afraid things would go badly with him. We must for that reason get track of him first, and in the meantime discover, if possible, the truth. Only then can we face a jury and clear him. And I can't help but think that when we do find him, we shall also discover that the letter which was supposed to have been written to Marion Paul when he sent her the necklace, was in reality intended for his wife. However, that is only theorising again. Now let us take the concrete fact of Fenmore's disappearance. He disappeared on the day after he had been cleaned out at Frileti's."

"Yes."

"If I am not mistaken, that same day was the day war was declared with Germany."

"That is true."

"Now, another element to be considered is this—Fenmore was practically penniless when he went away."

"'That is true also."

"When a man makes up his mind from some cause that he will disappear from his old haunts, a very necessary corollary to his going is his supply of cash. If he is an absconding bank cashier, he is usually well provided, and his thoughts at once turn to the United States or South America, or some other far country where he stands a fair chance of not being caught.

"If he is a crooked company promoter whose breach of the law is one which he can fight from a foreign country, he usually makes for the Continent or Morocco. But if he is just an individual who has done something which determined him to get out, and if he is not provided with funds, he takes the line of least resistance always. Now, in ordinary time that same line of least resistance is to get aboard a ship and endeavour to work one's way to some distant clime.

"But on the day Bob Fenmore disappeared things were not normal. They were very abnormal, and since we can only presume that he was not plentifully supplied with funds, we must further presume that he would come within the third category we have outlined. That is to say, he would take the line of least resistance. Now, since his name has cropped up in this case, I have gone back in my memory to try and remember some facts concerning him.

"Unfortunately, I have nothing regarding him in my Information Index. But I do remember that at the time of the South African War he served with the Forces, and I seem to recollect that he was mentioned for distinguished service. That brings us to the point where we can connect up matters to some extent. With war in the air, he was bound to be affected. No man who has ever been under fire could escape a stirring of the pulses and the call of the powder.

"Let us imagine Fenmore leaving home in a frame of mind which we can well imagine. He seeks escape from himself, and if he is filled with remorse, would probably welcome death. What, then, would he most likely do? Would he seek to get out to one of the colonies as he might in normal times? I do not think so!

"In my opinion he would go at once and endeavour to enlist. He might have to wait a day or two, but it is my opinion that Bob Fenmore would have been one of the first lot who took the King's shilling. I may be wrong, but I do not think so. Of course, if he did that, and went to the front, then, if we can find him, we can prove beyond doubt that he had nothing to do with the murder of his cousin. But we must find him first, and I am afraid it is not going to be an easy matter."

As he finished speaking, Blake leaned back. Yvonne sat in deep thought for some moments, then she asked a few questions to clear her mind of one or two puzzling points. Then she rose to depart, and when the door had closed after her, Blake returned to the desk.

"To think that it was she who took the necklace!" he murmured, with a smile. "I was positive that the owner of those small footprints could not have put up a severe struggle with a man as powerful as Craig must have been. I am very much afraid, inspector, that the charming Miss Paul has put you on the wrong scent. Now, I wonder if she did so with intention? I wonder. So Bob Fenmore is a father, eh?

"What a girl Yvonne is. She grows more whimsical and quixotic every day. All, well, only the future can tell the truth regarding this affair. Perhaps Tinker will be able to light on something of value. And in Yvonne I have acquired an unexpected and valuable assistant. Now, to make an examination of that rose petal, then to put in motion the machinery to find Bob Fenmore."

And as he spoke Blake once more picked up the petal and started towards the laboratory.

(1.) Half-way down the trench, sitting alone, and staring gloomily before him was a man for whom there had been no letter.

(2.) The khaki-clad figures scrambled over the lip of the trench, and with a hoarse cheer plunged towards the trenches of the Germans.

The Fourth Chapter.   Tinker Makes a Startling Discovery —The Enemy Strikes.

WHEN Tinker left Baker Street on his errand to Knightsbridge he had no idea as to what the surroundings of the hotel which was his objective were like. He only knew the name of the hotel from Blake and could not place it at all. Which was a peculiar thing with one who knew London as Tinker knew it. But as a matter of fact the place had only been recently turned into a private hotel, given over mostly to rather sumptuously furnished flats like the one which Marion Paul occupied. Previous to that it had been a private house of generous dimensions, and this made the change a matter of comparative simplicity.

So, when he finally reached it, Tinker saw that he knew the place after all. He remembered it as having been occupied in the past by a certain Member of Parliament with strong ambitions, and to further these he had given many large entertainments. But Fate had decreed that the plums of the political world should not be his, so when he had retired to the country in high dudgeon the house had been to let.

Almost across the street from it was another small hotel which Tinker surmised may have been the one at which Marion Paul and her maid stayed the previous night after the shocking discovery in the sitting-room. He was to find out a little later that his surmise was correct.

It was just on lunch time when he arrived, and since the chances were that he might have a long vigil he congratulated himself that he had had a bite in the City before returning to Baker Street.

He took up his position first just across the street from the hotel which he was to watch, leaving an examination of the rear of the premises until a more suitable chance should present itself. He was an expert at idling about without attracting attention, but, though he seemed to wander some distance from the place he was watching, it was, in reality, never out of his sight.

About one o'clock he saw the well-known figure of Inspector Thomas descend from a taxi and enter the hotel. Tinker had a strong desire to go after him and visit the flat in his company, for he had at times been of great assistance to the inspector, and he knew if he made the request that it would not be refused. But consideration told him that such a thing might be unwise. He knew Marion Paul very

84

well by sight, but she did not know him, and he thought it just as well that she shouldn't, since he was to watch her. And there was always the possibility that she might be in the flat at that moment.

So he contented himself with drawing a little nearer to the entrance and redoubling his vigilance.

It was close on two o'clock before the inspector emerged, but when he did he was not alone. With him were two men whom Tinker had no difficulty in recognising as plain clothes men. He remembered that Blake had said that there were two men on duty there, and later that he had prophesied the return of Marion Paul to the flat that day. It was now quite evident to him that the police were evacuating the place as his master had said they might do, and when they had driven off he immediately turned his attention to the other hotel where he had thought Marion Paul might be staying.

Sure enough, another half hour showed him to be right. At half-past two exactly he saw her issue forth from the place he was watching, and, in company with a woman whom he look to be her maid, walked across the street to the hotel where the murder had taken place.

Immediately behind them came a porter bearing some light luggage, and with this he disappeared into the hotel behind them. A moment later he reappeared thrusting something into his pocket, and it was evident to Tinker that he had been tipped and sent away.

Now that he knew definitely where his quarry was located things were much simplified for Tinker, because it was only necessary to watch one place, whereas before he had been compelled to give his attention to two. A solid hour dragged by without anything happening to attract his particular attention.

He was still idling up and down when, as he was standing in front of a shop window, which contained a large mirror in which was reflected the door of the hotel opposite, he noticed that a man had paused close beside him, and was apparently interested in the contents of the window. Tinker glanced at him casually and noted that he was obviously a French man.

After his first casual glance he was turning away again when the stranger moved a little closer, and while bending forward as though to get a better look at some object displayed within, said without moving his lips:

"It is just out on the bulletins that on account of what happened last night, Marion Paul will not appear on the stage for a week. So your work will be more strenuous as you won't have her placed at the theatre for the evening. See that you don't lose her for a moment. I am more keen than ever to know all she does and every place she goes. If necessary send for Tim to relieve you."

Then the "stranger" straightened up, and passed on as though his curiosity had been satisfied. Tinker never moved a muscle of his face, but as the tall figure moved away, he breathed:

"All right, guv'nor."

It was Blake, but not even Tinker had suspected his identity until he had spoken.

"Something must have developed since I left," mused the lad, as he turned back to his surveillance of the hotel. But he never dreamed for a moment that the development had been a long visit from Yvonne during which Blake had discovered a good many bits of information.

Still another hour went by, and then Marion Paul appeared dressed in a long fur coat, and wearing a thick veil. But it was not thick enough to hide her features from Tinker's sharp eyes, and when he saw the commissionaire come out to summon a taxi for her he looked about for one for himself.

In that quarter there was no dearth of them, and so, when she had entered one, and it was driving off towards Piccadilly, Tinker was clambering in one and directing the driver to follow the one ahead. Past Hyde Park Corner they went, and straight down Piccadilly until they came to Dover Street. There the leading taxi turned up and did not pause until it drew into the kerb almost across from Hay Hill. Tinker quickly signalled his driver to do likewise, and sat watching with a puzzled frown while Marion Paul descended and entered a building given over to flats.

"Now I wonder what she wants there," he soliloquised. "Unless I am mistaken those chambers are given over entirely to men. I guess I will just sling along and ask the constable on the corner. It looks like Jim Dennison. If it is, he will tell me what I want to know."

Suiting the action to the word Tinker descended from the taxi, and telling the man to wait, crossed the street to where the constable was standing. When he got near he saw that it was Dennison as he had thought, and he smiled as the constable turned:

"Hallo, Jim," he said cheerfully. "I didn't know you were on this beat. What is the matter with Ludgate Circus?"

Dennison smiled again.

"Hallo, Tinker. Nothing is the matter with the Circus. I just came up here to-day. What with the changes in duties and the drafting out of all the special constables we hardly know where we will be on duty from one day's end to another.

"Yes, lady, just down the hill to Berkeley Square." This as an old lady inquired the way of him.

"I say, Jim," went on Tinker, when the old lady had gone on her way, "what is that place over the way? I thought it only comprised men's chambers."

The constable looked at him in amazement.

"Why, where have you been since yesterday? That place is where the man who was murdered last night had his room."

"Oh, I see," said Tinker with a long whistle.

"Why, what is your reason for asking," went on the constable.

But he had addressed his words to the thin air for Tinker was already half way across the street heading for the entrance to the chambers.

"Now, that's funny," muttered the man in blue. "I wonder if he was getting at me. He is going in. I'll bet he only came up here to find that place. He is getting as deep as Blake himself."

With that he turned to answer another inquiry, and for the time being dismissed the matter from his mind.

Tinker had entered the place and in passing along the lower hall got hold of the porter. A long experience of the members of that profession had taught him that the yellow sheen of gold had a mighty power to move them, so before approaching this particular one with any questions he drew out a sovereign and twiddled it carelessly between his fingers.

"I suppose you have been harried to death with inquiries," he said by way of a beginning.

The porter gazed at Tinker with one eye, and at the gold with the other.

"If you are one of them reporter chaps you are late," he said, with a touch of impatience in his tones. "They have been pestering me for information all day, and there is nothing to tell them."

"But Craig, the man who was murdered, did live here, didn't he?" asked Tinker.

"Oh, yes, he lived here all right—him and his servant."

"There was a servant, was there? A man?"

"Yes, and you'll get no information out of him. There's been more than one tried that game to-day, but nary a one got his nose past the door. He has locked himself in and is packing up his late master's stuff."

"Did you see a lady come in here a few minutes ago?" queried Tinker, going off on a new tack.

"Yes, and I expected to see her down again before this."

"Why?"

"Because she went up to Mr. Craig's flat. I thought she must be one of those lady reporters you read about, though I never seed one before. But she must have got her foot in the door, because she is still there."

"What does the servant look like?" asked Tinker.

"Oh, he's one you could never miss, he is. He's got a big scar down one side of his face. I think he's a German or something like that, though he says he is British born. Anyway, when they rounded up all the alien enemies in London he escaped someway."

"I guess Mr. Craig fixed it for him. I see. It is evident that there is no love lost between you."

"Well, I haven't had no trouble with him, but I didn't fancy him too much."

Then Tinker risked a bold leap.

"I say, porter," he said in a low tone. "I am very anxious to have a look at that man and the woman who went up there. This sovereign is yours if you can fix it for me. I may tell you that I am not a reporter, but am working on a matter in which the Government is interested."

The porter scratched his head.

"I dunno how I can fix it," he replied, "though I won't deny that I could do with the money. There ain't no way of seeing into the flat, and that's where the woman must have gone since she hasn't come down, though how she persuaded him to admit her I don't know. Wait a minute. I've got an idea. I can't fix it for you to see into the flat, but if they are not standing at the door I can let you into the flat right across the hall from it. It is empty, and you can at least see them when she leaves."

"Good. That will be better than nothing. Here is the sovereign. Now take me up."

"Better come up in the lift, sir," said the porter. "Then, if they should be talking at the door, I can see them and keep on going to the next floor, then they won't suspect anything."

Tinker nodded and followed him to the lift. A moment later they were speeding upwards, and at the third floor the porter stopped.

"They are inside," he whispered. "Nip out now and I'll open the other door."

Tinker hopped out and tiptoed along to the door of the flat which was exactly opposite the one which Craig had occupied. It was a stroke of good fortune that it was unoccupied.

The porter followed him closely, and, drawing out a bunch of keys, fitted one in the lock. Then Tinker slipped within and closed the door softly. He waited until the lift had descended again before he began to reconnoitre.

As he had entered, he had noticed that over the door was a glass transom over which a curtain had been fitted. This seemed to offer some opportunity for watching the other flat, and at any rate he determined to test it.

Slipping through into the sitting-room of the flat he got a chair, and bringing it back to the hall set it in position close to the door. Then he stood on it and found that he had a perfect view of the door opposite. Resting his hands against the wall to steady himself he set himself to wait.

Five, ten, fifteen minutes went by before he saw anything, but when that space of time had elapsed the door opposite opened suddenly and Marion Paul appeared. She turned back to speak to someone as she reached the threshold, and then Tinker saw a man behind her. From the jagged scar which disfigured one side of his face he knew it was the dead man's servant. But what struck him most was Marion Paul's attitude. She was speaking to him in a very confidential way, and as an equal, while from time to time she kept tapping the bag which she carried.

The man nodded from time to time in response to her words, but, unfortunately, the glass was so thick that Tinker could not catch anything of what was said. But that Marion Paul was no stranger to the servant of the murdered man was very evident, and that they were on particularly intimate terms was even more evident.

After a few more minutes' earnest conversation the woman turned to depart, and the man closed the door.

Tinker waited until she had plenty of time to reach the ground floor; then he opened the door, and raced down the stairs after her. The porter was in the lower hall, and glanced up inquiringly as Tinker came down, but the lad only nodded and kept on.

When he reached the street he saw that Marion Paul had already entered her taxi, and that it was just drawing away from the kerb. Hurrying along to his own, he gave the man the same order as before, and they turned down Dover Street on the tail of the other.

Now the chase led down Piccadilly to Piccadilly Citrus, and thence into Shaftesbury Avenue, until the leading one turned to the left past a theatre. Up this street it went until it came to Greek Street, along which it continued for some distance. Then it drew up in front of a small bookshop whose speciality seemed to be second-hand books in foreign languages.

Had Tinker's taxi stopped close to the other, his reason would have been obvious, for the street was narrow, and for the moment there were no other cabs in that vicinity. So he signalled the driver to keep on and take the next turning to the left.

As soon as they had turned the corner Tinker rapped for him to pull up, and springing out he strolled back to the corner. His quarry was not in sight, so he concluded that she had descended and entered the bookshop before which her taxi had stopped.

Five minutes proved him to be right, for she emerged from the shop and re-entered the taxi. Tinker scurried back to his own, and ordered the man to get on the trail once more. They just caught the other as it turned back into Shaftesbury Avenue, and from there it was a clear chase back to Knightsbridge.

At her hotel Marion Paul descended and dismissed the cab. Tinker drove on a little distance, but when through the window at the rear he saw her enter the hotel, he too stopped and got out. After paying the driver, he strolled back towards the hotel and took up his position, cross the street.

It was now quite dark, for the December day had drawn to a close, and the hurrying throngs, with their packages, looked very like Christmas indeed. But Tinker was not thinking of the season at the moment; he was wondering what had been Marion Paul's object in visiting the flat of the man who had been murdered, and why she appeared to be on such intimate terms with his servant.

Then, too, he was racking his brains over her visit to the

bookshop in Greek Street. Of course, it was quite within the bounds of possibility that she had gone to the latter place merely to purchase some books, but the thing against that argument was that she had carried no parcel when she had emerged from the shop, and one doesn't usually ask little shops in the heart of Soho to send purchases to one's home.

He was debating, too, whether it would be safe to relax his watch in front for a bit, and make his way round to the rear in order to reconnoitre the position there against his intention for later in the evening.

As six o'clock drew round he decided to risk it, so crossing the street he dodged down a narrow side street, and kept on until he came to a lane which evidently served the hotel and the other buildings in that immediate vicinity for tradesmen's purposes.

It was very dark and silent along this, and he went forward with little risk of discovery, until he reached a spot which he knew must be immediately to the rear of the hotel. A high wall hid the yard from view, and when he tried the door which opened into it he found it secured by a heavy padlock. If it had been unfastened the previous night, the people in the hotel were evidently determined that such a thing should not occur again. But the wall was not an unsurmountable obstacle to one as active as Tinker, and when he used the handle of the door as a foothold it became comparatively easy for him to climb over.

He dropped to the ground on the other side, and stood for a moment in the shadow peering about him. Through the windows at the rear he could see the kitchens, and the servants busy preparing dinner. Above that was a brilliantly-lighted room which he took to be a dining-room for those who did not have their meals prepared in their own apartments. Then over that, again, was a dimly-lit room with drawn blinds, which he rightly concluded was the drawing-room. From that up it was easy to see that the rest of the building was given up to flats and apartments.

He moved cautiously over to the left, where he could see the dark bulk of the outbuildings which had been used to force an entry into Marion Paul's flat the night before. Standing close to them, he gazed upwards, and just over the line where the roof met the main building he saw the black oblong of a window.

"Now, that must be the kitchen window of her flat," he muttered to himself. "If it is, then it is not going to be very difficult getting into it. The trouble will be to keep from being discovered after I get in. But it is the window all right. The only other one where the outbuilding approaches is undoubtedly a drawing-room of some sort, and probably belongs to the hotel in general. Ah, there goes the light! It is a kitchen, and there comes the maid to draw the blind. And, by jingo, it is the same woman who walked across the street this afternoon with my quarry! That is the flat all right. She is probably going to prepare dinner now. At any rate, I think I will just climb up on the roof and risk a peep in the window."

He moved stealthily about until he found a firm foothold, then gripping the edge of the roof with both hands he swung himself up, landing easily. From the edge he crept up the slanting surface foot by foot, until he could almost touch the window-sill, and there he lay motionless for a few minutes.

At last he stirred and started to raise himself, when suddenly the window-blind was pushed aside, and he dropped flat as he saw the figure of the maid appear. At first he thought she must have heard him, but a moment later he heard the catch of the window closed, and realised that she had merely come to fasten it for the night.

The blind dropped a moment later, and he breathed easier. Then he raised himself again, and found that by resting on his knees he could see in beneath the blind, which was some two inches from the sill. The room on the other side was the kitchen, as he had suspected, and he could plainly see the maid as she busied herself over the table which was set against the opposite wall.

Tinker utilised the opportunity to make a mental note of the objects of the room and their position, and could even see a little distance along the hall to a door which he suspected from its position was the servant's bed-room, of which Blake had spoken, and which would be marked on the plan which his master had given him.

Then, even as he watched, he saw the light fall on something blue in the hall, and a moment later Marion Paul appeared, dressed in a soft house gown of a soft blue shade. She came into the kitchen and spoke a few words to the maid, and Tinker noticed the same peculiarity of manner which he had noticed at the chambers in Dover Street. The mistress spoke more to the maid as an equal than as an employee.

She turned and departed after a few words, and when she had

gone Tinker slipped back down the roof, and dropped lightly to the ground. He made his way to the wall at the rear, and climbing over walked slowly round to the main thoroughfare.

"One thing is certain," he muttered, as he took up his old stand. "She doesn't intend going out before dinner, otherwise she wouldn't be dressed in that kind of an affair. Since she is not going to the theatre, she may be intending to stay in this evening. Perhaps she will have someone call. At any rate, just as soon as it is safe I am going to tackle that roof again, and if I can't push back that silly old catch on the window then my name is Mike. She will probably dine somewhere between seven and half-past eight. I guess it will be safe enough for me to slip along the street and get something to eat myself. I will find a place near here, and can get back on the job by half-past seven. I may have to stick it out till midnight, or after, and if anything should develop after that I might be going till morning before I get a chance to get back to report to the guv'nor."

Suiting the action to the thought, he strolled along until he came to a small restaurant about another block down, and entering, ordered dinner.

It was just on half-past seven when he finished and made his way back to his post of observation. He hung about in the main street for another half-hour, then darting across to the other side he slipped along the side street to the lane at the rear where he had been before. Here he adopted the same tactics which had been his earlier, and getting over the high wall moved across the yard to the shadow of the outhouses.

Standing there, he could look up and see an orange glow behind the drawn blind, and from this he knew that the servant must still be in the kitchen.

In the basement of the hotel itself he could see the servants hurrying about, and from this it was obvious that dinner was just progressing in the hostelry. He realised it was entirely possible that some errand might bring one of the hotel servants into the yard at any moment, and for purposes of concealment he figured the roof of the outbuilding to be as safe a place as any.

At any rate, he determined to use it as one, so once again he looked for a foothold, and swung himself up. He crept as cautiously as possible up the sloping roof, until he could almost touch the sill of the kitchen window. Here he crouched for some minutes perfectly motionless, in order to discover if he could hear any movements in the room beyond the window.

Not a sound greeted his ears, so at the end of another five minutes he risked a peep. Resting on his knees as he had before, he raised himself until his eyes were just above the level of the sill, then he leaned forward.

Sitting at the table which was placed against the opposite wall he could see the maid-servant. She was eating her dinner and reading an evening paper at the same time. Tinker felt a keen curiosity to know what particular bit of news interested her at the moment, and bending still closer he was able to distinguish which evening paper it was.

As chance would have it, he had read this same journal while eating his own dinner in the restaurant down the street, and when he spied the column which held her eye he was certain it was about the murder the previous night. Now he wondered if that fact might indicate anything in the line of his investigations.

After pondering on the matter he was reluctantly compelled to put it aside as being of no definite use at the moment, for it was quite reasonable that a maid-servant in the hotel where the murder had taken place, and particularly the maid of the flat, which had seen it, would be all agog to learn the latest developments.

Just then the faint tinkle of a bell inside caught Tinker's ear, and he saw the maid rise at once. She did not leave the room immediately, but, going to the stove, took off a large coffee-pot. The coffee service itself was on a small table at the side, and now she filled the small pot which was on the tray. Then putting the larger one back on the stove, she took up the tray and left the kitchen. Tinker watched her as she disappeared along the hall, then, quickly diving into his pocket, he drew out a strong pocket-knife. He hastily opened the blade of this, and began to insert it upwards between the upper and lower sashes of the window.

"Might as well do it now while I have the chance," he muttered. "If it does make a little noise now, and she should hear it, she will only think it is something in the kitchen, whereas if she had cleaned up and left, and they should hear the noise inside when everything was quiet, it might arouse suspicion, especially after what happened, last night."

While he muttered to himself he was working away, and suddenly there was a sharp click as the catch shot back.

"Good." he breathed. "That fixes that part, anyway. Now, I suppose, I must wait here until she cleans up."

At that moment the maid returned, bearing a large tray of plates and other implements of the table. Tinker watched her savagely while she proceeded to scrape them and arrange them for washing, and realising that she would be some time at least, he slid back down the roof, and following his old method made his way back to the main street. Here in the light cast by a corner lamp he drew out the rough plan of the flat with which Blake had provided him, and began to study it in detail.

"Now, that is the guest-room of which the guv'nor spoke," he muttered, putting his finger on the room which was indicated as being off the branch hall and just opposite the study. "That would be the passage of which I can see a part from the window at the rear," he went on. "At the very end of this hall and to the left as I see along it must be the dining-room. That is where Marion Paul is now. The question is, has she company or is she alone? There have been several people passed into the hotel, but I am hanged if I know whether any of them have been going to see her!

"Perhaps I can tell that later. If she is alone the chances are she will go to the study and sit in there. If she has a guest, and is intimate with them, she will probably do the same thing. But if she should have a guest who was a stranger, or with whom she was not on familiar terms, she would probably take them into the sitting-room at the front. No, she wouldn't either. She wouldn't be likely to sit in the room where the murder took place.

"If she took a guest to the front of the house to sit she would probably take them to her own boudoir. But on the whole, I think she would choose the smoking-room or study, whichever she calls it. If that should be so then the place I must manage to get is into the guest-room just opposite it. Hang that maid, I wonder if she will stick around in kitchen all evening or go to her own room. If she does the first my plans will be cooked, but if she does the second I might manage to creep past her door without being heard. Anyway, I must risk it if there is a possible chance of bringing it off."

So saying he folded up the plan and stuffed it back into his pocket. Then he turned and leisurely made his way back to the yard of the hotel. Just as he got over the wall, and was starting across the bit of yard between it and the outbuilding, which was his objective, the rear door of the hotel flew open without the slightest warning and a man came out.

Tinker's heart gave a great bound, and he sprang back into the shadow and dropped flat to the ground as the man came straight towards him. The door had not been closed, and his figure was silhouetted against it as he came forward.

Tinker felt certain he must have been seen, so straight was the man coming, and, as he drew still nearer, the lad gathered himself together for quick flight. It seemed strange that the other said nothing and made no attempt to summon any of his fellows who might be within call.

But when he had drawn to within a few feet of the lad he turned suddenly to the right, and then Tinker saw that he was carrying a pail of rubbish, and in the same moment he realised that the man could probably see very little in the yard, for he would still be half blinded from the glare of the lights in the kitchen.

Tinker lay close to the wall, scarcely breathing, until the man had dumped his pail of rubbish and betaken himself back to the kitchen. When the door had closed with a slam the lad sprang to his feet and darted across to the outbuilding.

Once more he swung himself up to the roof and crept along to his old position. But his experience in the yard had taught him to be careful of not showing his own silhouette against the window beneath which he lay. A cautious peep showed him that the maid had almost finished her cleaning up, and for another quarter of an hour he watched her impatiently.

Finally, however, she had completed her task, and he saw, with relief, that she was preparing to extinguish the light.

He waited until she had done so, then for a moment he could catch a gleam of light which fell out into the hall from a room farther up the passage—a room which he judged to be the study.

Suddenly, he could see it no longer, and even as he puzzled over the phenomenon the explanation struck him. The maid had left the kitchen, and in going had closed the kitchen door. So much the better for his plans. He gave another quarter of an hour to caution, then, raising himself a little more, he began to work gently at the sash of the window.

Ever so slowly it moved upwards until there was a space of about half an inch between the sill and the lower frame of the sash. Now he worked his fingers through this opening in order to get a better leverage, and, exerting a steady pressure, he had the satisfaction of seeing the sash go up inch by inch without any perceptible noise.

Higher and higher he pushed it until there was room for his body to squeeze through, then he desisted, and, with infinite caution, worked one leg over the sill. Another minute and he was standing inside the kitchen.

Before making another move he stood listening. The low murmur of voices came to him from somewhere up the hall, and from time to time he caught the deep timbre of a man's tones.

Evidently Marion Paul had had a guest to dinner, as he had half expected might be the case. When he felt satisfied that his entry had been unsuspected, he turned and softly closed the window again in case the maid should happen to return to the kitchen on some errand or other. Then he sat down on the floor, and from one of his pockets drew a pair of heavy woollen socks. These he pulled on over his boots in order to deaden the sound of his movements, and now, having provided as far as possible against discovery, he tiptoed across to the door which opened into the hall.

Although the maid had drawn it to she had not slammed it, and it was not closed tight. It only required to be drawn back gently, and, as he began to do so, Tinker held himself tense for fear it might squeak. But luck was with him, for it made not the slightest sound. Now he could see along the hall, and noticed that the murmur of voices was coming from the study, the door of which appeared to be almost closed.

He made a step forward and stood close to the wall on his right in order to get a look at the door of the guest-room, and unconsciously nodded his head with satisfaction as he saw that it was partially open. The door of the maids' room was very close to him now, but it was closed, and he could not see whether there was a light in it or not.

It took no little nerve to make the start towards the guestroom, which was his immediate objective, for he did not know much about the inhabitants of the flat, and could not guess what might happen were he discovered. And to make matters even more risky he had the maid to guard against. She might pop out on him at any moment. But he realised that it would be a big advance in his investigations should he succeed in his attempt, so, taking his courage and his caution in his hands, he essayed the first step along the hall.

Then came the second and the third, and so he went on, drawing nearer each moment to his goal.

Foot by foot and yard by yard he made the distance until his hand was almost at the door of the guest-room. Now the voices from the study reached him quite plainly, and from the few words he caught he realised that an earnest discussion of some sort was in progress.

But he dared not risk standing there for long, so, moving with the same caution which had characterised the first part of his journey, he reached the door of the guest-room and slipped inside. Once there he breathed more freely, but scarcely had he gained his coveted point of vantage when the door of the study opened, and, peering forth, he saw the maid come out.

She went towards the kitchen, but as she had not closed the door of the study after her Tinker had a perfect view of the interior. He saw a smallish room which was, as Blake had said, a sort of study and smoking-room combined. It was decorated and furnished in the style known as Nouveau Art, and the prevailing impression was one of orange and black with an elusive touch of Orientalism about the whole thing.

In the very centre of the room, and straight within his line of vision, was a large, peculiarly-shaped table at which sat three people. A chair which had been pushed back from the side nearest the door showed where the maid must have been sitting.

Facing Tinker, and still gowned in the pale-blue house gown which he had seen before, was Marion Paul. A little thrill went through Tinker as he saw that the man on her left was he of the jagged scar on whom she had called that afternoon. On her right was a short, stout man of Teutonic cast of countenance and of about middle age. He wore spectacles with extra large lenses of a bluish tinge, and at the moment appeared to be dominating the conversation.

Every word reached Tinker clearly, but at present they were speaking of trivialities. He wondered who the bespectacled individual might be. Of one thing he was certain, and that was that he had never seen him before.

He could not help wondering what sort of business it was which had caused Marion Paul to call on the dead man's servant, and later to sit at the table with him apparently on the most intimate terms.

And the presence of her own maid at the gathering, which seemed to be a conference of some sort, needed explaining, too.

Just then Tinker heard a step in the hall, and he saw the maid reappear with a box of matches in her hand. Evidently the soothing power of nicotine was to be introduced into the deliberations.

When the maid re-entered the room she almost closed the door after her, and when he heard her draw her chair up to the table Tinker dropped to his knees and thrust his head outside the door of the room where he had concealed himself. There was a striking of matches, then the heavy odour of Turkish tobacco came to him, followed by the low rumble of a voice which he took to be that of the Teutonic-looking one. In reply to what was evidently a question he heard the clear accents of Marion Paul, and noted that they were somewhat impatient.

"I can't see why you ask that again," she was saying. "I should never have sent for you or Max if the situation had not demanded it. I realise exactly how dangerous it is for you to show yourself, but the situation is such that I do not feel like coping with it alone. We must decide without delay what it is best to do. I went to see Max to-day before I sent word to you, and he agrees with me that a conference is essential."

"Well," came the rumbling tones. "Tell me everything and then I can advise what is best to be done."

"I have already told you the chief point of danger, and while that exists I tell you frankly I don't feel like brazening out things here."

"You mean the entry of Sexton Blake into the affair?"

"Of course—what else?"

"I agree with you, my dear Marion, that he is an element of danger, but so carefully have our plans been laid that I do not think he will ever drop on anything to connect you with the affair."

"I am not so sure of that," she replied. "I have heard so much about his almost uncanny faculty for getting at things that I am nervous. When he was here this morning he seemed to look at me as though he knew all about it, and when he coolly appropriated the letter I was forced to show him I simply didn't dare ask for it back. Nor did I dare to trust myself in the flat a moment longer. I was frightened of him, and I have never felt that way in my life before."

"You were nerved up after last night," replied the man, soothingly. "It was a bigger strain on you than you thought, and you see danger everywhere. But I shouldn't worry about this man Blake. He has had some good luck in his cases, and there is a sort of impression about that he is infallible. But his is not the only clever mind in the world, and if he can ferret out the truth about last night he is much cleverer than I think."

"But if he hadn't suspected something about that letter why did he keep it?" objected Marion Paul.

There was a short silence, then the man said:

"That is a question I can't answer, my dear, but it may have been because he wanted some writing in the hand of Fenmore in order to assist him to find that individual. There seems to be no doubt that the police suspect him after hearing your story."

"Oh, the police!" she said irritably. "I am not worrying about them. They may be sure, but the red tape by which they are bound makes them slow, and one has a chance to act in case of necessity. But this man Sexton Blake is not bound by any rules. He works off his own bat, and you know as well as I do that sometimes he gets results very quickly. Not only that, but I have also noticed that the police usually act promptly on any of his suggestions."

"Oh, I know all that, my dear, but that doesn't prove that we have cause to fear him at present!"

"You may be right, Johann, but some intuition tells me you are wrong in this instance."

To the listening Tinker, who was straining every nerve to catch every word that was said, this conversation was startling. He had had little idea why Blake was so keen for him to gain access to the flat, and until then he had only vaguely gathered that Marion Paul was suspected of knowing more of the events of the previous night than she had acknowledged to the police.

But now it was beginning to dawn on him that she knew a very great deal, and that she had been sharp enough to see the menace caused by the entry of Blake into the case. What may have gone before Tinker had no idea, but from what had just been said he gathered that Marion Paul had summoned the gathering because, in her own words, she "was frightened." Of Blake? It seemed so. And the bespectacled individual whom she called Johann was evidently trying to calm her fears. But what had she to fear? Did she actually know who had committed the crime? And was she endeavouring to shield them?

If that supposition were so then all four who were in that room must know. Then did that mean that they had made the plans? Why—

and Tinker almost gasped audibly as the thought came to him—if that were so, then one of that very four might be the murderer of Harold Craig.

But a moment later he was puzzled still more, for a new voice broke in which he took to be that of the late Craig's servant.

"What I think we have the most to fear from," he said slowly, "is not Sexton Blake but the unknown individual who entered the flat last night and got away with the Fenmore necklace. What puzzles me is this: How did the thief know Marion wasn't wearing it last night? It was the first time for weeks she had gone without it, and that was only because of our own plans. But now she says that when Zela looked in the safe last night it was gone, and this morning Marion had to appear surprised as intended without knowing what had actually become of it."

Then came another voice, and this Tinker took to be that of the maid whose name was evidently Zela.

"Max is right," she said. "I think as he does about that. I say too, what has become of the necklace? Whoever took it knew quite well it was there last night. But what strikes me as even more of a danger is this: Did that unknown person enter the flat before or after Craig's arrival? If the thief entered before he must have seen that the room was upset, and would also see that there was nobody there! If he came in after then he would see the body and know something was wrong. He would be almost certain to go over and look at the body, and if he did he would be almost certainly overcome by the flowers. That is what puzzles me. Whoever it was has probably read the papers, and that means there is an individual in London to-night who knows a good deal more of the affair than is healthy for us that he should."

"Zela is right," broke in Marion Paul excitedly. "I tell you, Johann, we have bungled this affair. If you had left Craig to me a little longer I should have arranged something better. But your infernal jealousy must get the better of you and run us all into a hole."

"It won't do you any good to talk that way," replied the man called Johann. "Craig was no more useful to us. You had got everything out of him which was possible to get, and he was getting dangerous. But wait—by Heavens, I have an idea!"

"What is it?" asked Marion Paul eagerly.

"It has just occurred to me that Craig himself might have been the one who took the necklace. When you asked him to come on here and get things ready for supper later you told him you would give him back the necklace, didn't you?"

"Of course. You know that was the chief reason he came. I doubt if he would have come at all had I not promised that. He was worrying me all day about it. But what do you suggest?"

"Did anyone go through his pockets before the police came?"

"Not that I know of, and I didn't see them go through them. But if you suggest that Craig opened the safe when he first entered and took out the necklace before he went to pick up the flowers and put the room to rights you are on the wrong track."

"Why?"

"Because if that were so, how about the next morning when I told the inspector that the necklace was missing? He would have known had it been found on Craig, and considering the fact that he looked upon me as the owner of it he would have told me at once."

"Yes, you are right," responded the man in a tone of regret.

"I never thought of that. I see that such a theory is impossible, and that means there is danger in the unknown thief as Max and Zela suggest. I don't know whether you three are talking soundly or whether you have simply affected me with your fears, but I am beginning to agree with you that we must tread very warily. But, whatever is done now must be done by you. I can plan for you and advise you, but you know it is next to impossible for me to go about. If the police dreamed I was at large in London they would have me sent to a camp of concentration in no time. Or since I did not report myself as I should have done, they would probably give me a term in prison, though thank goodness the London police have nothing else against me, and they certainly don't care now whether I am wanted in Berlin and Vienna or not. But we have started on this thing and we might as well go through with it. Now, shall I tell you what I would suggest as our next move?"

"Yes!" came the voices of the other three.

"First, I should say it was all important that we find the unknown thief who took the necklace and endeavour to get it back. Once we know whom it is we can soon take measures to silence him."

"But how shall we go about it?"

"Oh, I have thought of that. If we put a guarded notice in most of the morning papers he is almost sure to see it, and then we can arrange a meeting. Once we know the identity and arrange a meeting—well, I think I can guarantee that we shan't have any further worry on that score. I shall compose a notice to-night and see that it goes in the papers to-morrow morning. It must be written so no one but the thief will guess to what it refers. Now the second suggestion I have to make is about this man Sexton Blake. Draw in closer and I will tell you."

Then began a whispered conversation which, strain as he might, Tinker could not catch. But from what he had already heard he did not doubt but that the suggestion the man called Johann was now putting forward held a supreme menace for his master.

Just then he became conscious that there was a faint sniffing noise in the hall to his left, and as he listened to it he realised that it was drawing steadily closer. Then suddenly as he peered out he saw a little Pekingese spaniel trotting towards him. It stopped just outside the door and regarded him with hostile eyes, turning its head slowly in the direction of the other door as the sound of the whispering reached it.

After standing as though in thought for a moment it turned back to Tinker, and jumping away from him began to bark shrilly and persistently. There was the sudden pushing back of a chair in the other room, and Marion Paul's voice could be heard calling:

"Liyi! Liyi! Come here, you naughty fellow!"

Tinker realising the danger this contretemps had caused slipped farther back into the room and sought for a place of concealment. This move on his part was fatal, as he was to find out very soon.

The spaniel had had its curiosity aroused, and instead of going to its mistress when she called him made to follow Tinker into the room.

Had he had a chance he would have throttled the little beast gladly, and he did go so far as to make one dive for it. But it was too nimble for him, and the result of his effort was only to make it bark more excitedly than ever.

"What on earth can be the matter with the dog?" he heard one of the men say, then there was a rustling sound as the door of the study opened and Marion Paul came out calling dog.

"Why!" she exclaimed, "he has gone into the guest-room. Get a stick or something, Zola. He may be after a mouse."

She started to enter the room as she spoke, and Tinker realising that he was in imminent danger of discovery, poised himself ready to make a dash for it. His only chance now was to do what he should have done when the dog first appeared— race for the kitchen and endeavour to get through the window before he was overtaken. Once he could accomplish that he would be able to get away.

As the door was pushed open he decided that the moment to act had come, so gathering himself together he gave a loud yell in order to startle Marion Paul and make her draw back, then he started at full speed.

But the curious behaviour of the dog had brought the two men to their feet also, and the moment Tinker gave this yell both of them leaped forward. The result was that they and Tinker met in full collision in the hall between the two rooms, and all three went down with a fearful crash.

The lad gave himself a twist and endeavoured to leap to his feet before the others had recovered, but whatever Marion Paul was she was not a coward, and just as the lad was rising she threw her arms about his neck and sagged her full weight upon him.

He gave a vicious jerk which threw her back against the wall, but the delay had been fatal to him, for now the two men had scrambled up and were upon him with the savageness of a pair of tigers.

Tinker knew now that his plight was desperate, and unless he managed to outwit them very quickly he would be in a very serious position. A throb of uneasiness went through him as across his mind flashed the conversation he had just heard, for he knew that the quartette into whose hands he had fallen would stop at little to ensure safety for themselves.

Therefore, he fought with all his strength. Now that the two men had grappled with him Marion Paul evidently thought that they could easily handle him, for she took no further part in it.

But Tinker was not so easy to dispose of as she thought. He was as tough as nails and as wiry as a panther, and when his natural quickness was added to these it made a combination in which more than once had carried him through a tight place.

Had he only had the elder man to deal with he could have disposed of him easily, but the one who had posed as Craig's servant was no mean antagonist, and towards him Tinker exerted his greatest strength. By a lucky chance he caught the elder man a terrific blow in the pit of the stomach and sent him down with a grunt, but the moment necessary to do it had given the other one a temporary ad vatu use, and as Tinker turned to meet him he was caught by a straight left which sent him staggering into the study.

His assailant was upon him like a flash, and they went down together fighting like wild cats. Even now sheer nerve and speed might have carried Tinker through, but what he lacked in strength the man called Johann made up in cunning, and while he struggled on the floor for the advantage, Tinker did not see him take from his pocket a small bottle and saturate a handkerchief with the contents.

Then he sprang forward, and even as the lad was bending back his antagonist's head preparatory to making a leap for safety, he was caught round the neck from behind and the handkerchief pressed over his mouth and nose. A great wave of sickness swept through him, and realising that he was in danger of being chloroformed, he released his hold on the man beneath him and struggled to rise. But he was the fraction of a second too late, and even as he staggered to his feet his limbs suddenly gave way and he collapsed on the floor in a lifeless heap.

The Fifth Chapter.   The Secret Service Commission.

WHILE Tinker had been away on his investigation of things at Marion Paul's flat, Blake himself had not been idle, as witness, for instance, his seeking of the lad in the disguise of a foreigner, and the warning he gave him about the decision of the actress not to appear on the stage for a week.

This bit of information had come to Blake by accident, and he had lost no time in passing it on to Tinker. When Yvonne had come it will be remembered that Blake took up the rose petal from the desk for the purpose of examining it. This time he took no risks with such a dangerous specimen, but, holding it at arm's-length, made his way to the laboratory.

There he laid it on the experimenting table while he donned a protective mask, and, taking the precaution to put on a pair of rubber gloves, picked it up now with little danger to himself.

He had found out from Tinker what symptoms he had shown while under the influence of the poison with which the petal had undoubtedly been sprayed, and had taken note that his own condition must have been very similar to that of the man who had gone to his death through the same medium.

It had served to indicate to him a certain line of thought regarding the identity of the poison, and by the time he had reached the laboratory, he had formed a tentative theory as to the nature of it.

He was able to narrow down the field of investigation to very few known poisons, for the number which would serve as a spray and keep their strength for such a time must be limited indeed.

Then there was the extremely powerful nature to be considered as well as the immediate effect it had on the human system. If those few drops on a single petal could retain sufficient strength to be dangerous after nearly twenty-four hours had elapsed, then it must be of a particularly powerful nature.

His extensive knowledge of poisons of all kinds was naturally of great assistance to Blake in the present instance, and when he had laid the petal out for a thorough examination, he walked to a bookcase in the corner, and without the slightest hesitation, drew out a small blue volume.

"Unless I am greatly mistaken in my ideas, I shall get track of it in this," he murmured, as he returned to the experimenting-table.

Laying the book down, he opened it, and spent some few minutes studying the index.

Finally, he placed his finger on a line very near the end, and noting the number of the page indicated, turned the leaves until he came to it. The page was divided into three tables, and headed: "Poisons for Inhalation." In the first column was given the name of the poison, in the second the ingredients. and in the third, which was headed "Remarks," there was indicated the time it took the poison to act, the effect of it in doses of different sizes, the usual methods by which it was administered—as gathered from research—and a host of other notations which had been collected from different sources, last of all coming the different methods by which its presence might be detected, and stating when known what would counteract its effect.

These columns Blake studied for some time in deep absorption, then, taking up a pencil which lay near at hand, he ticked two of the names with it. Then he pushed the book from him, and searched about on the shelves above him until he found a small bottle quite full of a fine green powder.

Handling this with the utmost caution, for it was a powerful poison itself; he took out the stopper and shook a little on the rose petal. Replacing the stopper, he put the bottle back on the shelf, and turned back to the petal.

There was no change of any description to be seen, but evidently Blake expected none for the moment. He placed a glass cover over it, and walked to the other side of the room, where he busied himself with some instruments for a few minutes. When about five had gone, he walked back to the experimenting-table, and gazed at the petal. No change had taken place yet, and now he shook his head with disappointment.

"It is not that," he muttered, "and I can only see one more possible in the list. I'll try it, anyway. If it is not the second, then I can only conclude that I am up against a new poison. And that will at least be interesting."

He removed the glass cover, and, taking up the petal carefully, dusted the green powder off it on to the experimenting-table. Then he laid the petal to one side, and, lighting a match, stood well back while he applied the flame to the powder. There was a momentary flash as he did so, followed by a tiny wraith of smoke and the powder was no more.

Now he went to the shelves again, and took down a bottle of colourless liquid, which he handled almost as carefully as he had the powder. Setting it down, he reached for a small syringe, and taking off the bulb, poured a little in the glass tube. Then he replaced the stopper in the bottle, fixed the bulb on again, and prepared once more to test the petal.

Bending close over it, he sprayed it very gently, and when it was quite saturated laid the bulb aside. A change was not long in manifesting itself, for scarcely had he turned to it when a fine vapour began to rise. It was almost though that thin, tenuous wraith were eating away the very soul of the petal as it rose on the still air of the laboratory ever so slowly the rich crimson colour began to fade until the petal was only a tawdry-looking wisp of a dirty yellow.

But the bluish spots had also been affected by the spray, and now revealed themselves as patches of black as though an invisible hand had shaken drops of ink upon them.

And this time Blake smiled with satisfaction, for the test had proved, and he now knew beyond the shadow of a doubt exactly what deadly stuff had been sprayed on the roses in the sitting-room of the flat where Harold Craig had met his death.

And with the realisation of the nature of the poison, he understood better than ever how narrow his own escape had been.

He laid the petal away in a small specimen-box, and drawing towards him a notebook, began to write in the date, the nature of the specimen upon which he had experimented where he had found it, and how the effect it had had upon himself, and lastly, a full description of the method he had followed in order to identify it.

Then he locked the little book away, and returned to the consulting-room.

One step at least had been accomplished to his satisfaction. The first thing he did on entering the consulting-room was to telephone to a certain office in the City where he knew he was almost certain to find a man who, on occasions, did some valuable work for him. As he hoped, the man was there, and in a very few words Blake told him what he had to do.

"I want you," he said, "to go at once and endeavour to find out if the following man has enlisted in any of the services since the beginning of the war. You might also examine all the names of those granted commissions. I don't think he will be found there, and I doubt if you get track of him at all, for it was quite possible that if he did enlist he changed his name. The name is Fenmore—Robert Fenmore. What? Yes, that is the man. You needn't look at any records which were made before the declaration of war. Find out what you can, and let me know as soon as possible. Yes, here at Baker Street."

Then he closed off, and walked slowly to the window. But scarcely had he reached it, when the telephone rang shrilly, and he hurried back to the desk.

"Hallo, hallo!" he said. "Yes, this is Sexton Blake. What? Yes—oh, yes! I shall be there in twenty minutes!"

He rang off again, and as he went to get his hat and coat, muttered:

"The Secret Service want me again, eh? I suppose that means another rush trip to the Continent. If so, I shall have to drop this case and go at once!"

He bit off the end of a cigar as he walked to the door, and, pausing on the steps outside long enough to light it, glanced round as he did so for a taxi. One was coming slowly along on the opposite side, so, signalling to it, he walked to the kerb.

It drew up a moment later, and, giving the address of the Secret Service in Whitehall, he entered and leaned back, smoking thoughtfully, and thinking of the case he had just been working on.

But once he got to Whitehall, he put it sharply from him, and gave his mind entirely to the business in hand. That business, he discovered in a very few minutes, meant a rush trip to the Continent that very night in order to take over some particularly urgent despatches.

As the nation had the first call on his services, there was nothing for him to do but to get ready without delay, and to leave everything in abeyance until his return.

He drove straight back to Baker Street, and sat down at the desk in order to decide what was the best thing to be done.

It was still afternoon, so he thought it as well to go along and advise Tinker that he was going to the Continent. As the idea struck him, he jumped up and entered the dressing-room, and in less than twenty minutes he emerged in the disguise of a Frenchman as Tinker saw him a little later. Then he went out again, and, hailing another taxi, ordered the man drive him to Knightsbridge.

On the way, he saw the placards of the evening papers, and

noticed that one and all made a great headline of the fact that Marion Paul had announced that she would not appear on the stage for a week. He descended at Knightsbridge, and dismissing the taxi, walked slowly along, keeping his eyes open for Tinker.

It has already been seen how he warned the lad about Marion Paul, but, owing to the fact that two women pushed close to him just as he was speaking to the lad, he was forced to walk on without telling Tinker of his projected trip to the Continent. And because he thought it bad policy to again approach the lad while he was on watch, he did not return, but, calling another taxi, returned to Baker Street.

Since he was almost certain to be home again the next day, it really did not matter very much, and in any event he would leave a note for the lad explaining his absence.

But he would have to leave some kind of word for Yvonne, and the question was how best to get it to her. Blake realised only too well that there was a keen, shrewd brain behind the murder of Harold Craig, and he didn't propose for a moment to make any unnecessary parade of his interest in the matter.

Past experience had taught him that the detective who permits the enemy to know how he is working, when he is working, and with whom he is working, is rarely the one who gets results. And since Yvonne was probably so far unknown in the matter, he did not wish that she should become known to the enemy, whoever that might be.

The best plan seemed to be to utilise the telephone, and he was just about to pick up the book to look up the number of Mrs. Fenmore's flat, when the telephone rang once again. To his surprise, it was Yvonne herself.

"I called you up about half an hour ago," she said, "but you were evidently out, for I could get no answer."

"I was out," he replied. "I had to go to Whitehall. And it is an odd coincidence that at the very moment when the 'phone rang I was about to call you. I presume you rang up about that matter of which we were speaking?"

"Yes; that and something else. I have made inquiries here, and Bayles, the valet, tells me that Mr. Craig was here with Bob Fenmore on the morning the latter disappeared. That seems to be what you suspected, and also points to the possibility of Craig having had something to do with the necklace, don't you think?"

"It is exactly what I thought might be the case," replied Blake. "That letter had something strange about it. When I first read it I could not believe that it had been intended for Marion Paul, and now I feel sure we will eventually prove our point. What was the other thing about which you wished to speak to me?"

"Only that a funny thing happened a few moments ago. Have you missed anything?"

Blake knit his brows in puzzlement.

"Missed anything?" he echoed. "No, not that I know of. Why do you ask?"

Yvonne laughed. "I will tell you. I had occasion to go to the door a few moments ago, and when I opened it, what do you suppose I saw?"

"I can't guess."

"I saw Pedro calmly sitting on the step and apparently waiting to be let in. He must have followed me home. I have had him in the house, and I don't know if you are aware of the fact, but he is awfully fond of chocolate-creams. He has eaten I don't know how many!"

Blake smiled.

"I can see where he is on the road to being spoiled," he said. "You had better send him home. I hadn't noticed that he was not here. I thought he must be about the house somewhere."

"I have tried to persuade him to go, but he absolutely refuses. Shall I bring him round, or will you send for him?"

"Oh, wait a minute!" said Blake quickly. "Is he a nuisance to you?"

"No, indeed! I love having him here!"

"Then I wonder if you would mind keeping him until tomorrow? I have to leave for the Continent to-night. I will be back to-morrow, I expect. But Tinker is not here now, and I am afraid he will not be back until this evening."

"Of course I will keep him with pleasure. Have you anything for me to do while you are away?"

"Nothing, unless you care to come here this evening and wait for Tinker's return. He will turn up some time before midnight, I feel sure, and in case anything important has developed, he and you might attend to it. You could bring Pedro back then."

"All right. I will get away from here about eleven and go round. I presume you will leave at nine o'clock?"

"Yes; I shall catch that train. By the way, how is Mrs. Fenmore progressing?"

"Oh, she is doing as well as can be expected, but it makes my heart ache to hear her keep calling for her husband to return. I wish you could manage to locate him."

"I have started the machinery in motion already," replied Blake. "I do not know what success we will have, but I shall do my best, and while I am on the Continent I shall also endeavour to locate him if he should happen to be there. Don't worry. Everything will come out all right eventually."

"I hope so," she responded, and after a few more words they closed off.

That finished, Blake sent for Mrs. Bardell, and told her to pack a bag in readiness for his journey.

Then he had a hasty meal served in the consulting-room, and afterwards busied himself until about half-past seven with one or two matters of some import, but having no connection with the case he had in hand. At seven-thirty sharp, the phone rang again, and when he lifted off the receiver he recognised the tones of his agent in the City.

"I have investigated that matter, Mr. Blake. I put half a dozen assistants on it at once," he said.

"Yes," replied Blake, "and what have you discovered?"

"Absolutely nothing. I can't get a trace of the man having enlisted since the beginning of the war."

"All right, Adams," responded Blake "I hardly expected that you would. But keep your eyes open, and see if you can discover anything. If you do, let me know at once."

"I shall," answered the other.

Blake rang off and went at once to the desk. Seating himself, he wrote a hurried note to Tinker, telling him that Yvonne might turn up some time during the evening, that she was acquainted with all the facts of the case, and that he was to discuss with her any discoveries he had made so that they might take action together in his absence.

Then adding that he expected to be home the following night or the morning after at latest, he sealed it, and walking to the mantel, placed it in the interior of a small Eastern god where Tinker would be certain to look if he arrived home and found Blake not there.

That done, he donned a heavy travelling-coat, and, picking up his bag, made for the street. Hailing a taxi, he drove straight to Whitehall, where he was expected, and, after waiting there the best part of an hour, finally received the despatches which he was to take to the Continent and hand over to a messenger who was to meet him in Calais.

It was after half-past eight when he at last got started for Charing Cross, and as he entered the train their he little dreamed that Tinker was at the same moment creeping up the hall of Marion Paul's flat on a daring entry which was to lead him into deadly peril before that night was over.

Blake dozed nearly the whole way to Dover, and there found that the special boat which was to hurry him across to Calais was none other than the Fleur-de-Lys which Yvonne had handed over to the Admiralty, and which until a day or two before she herself had had command of.

Captain Vaughan and Hendricks, the mate, welcomed him cordially, and conducted him to the beautiful saloon, where an appetising supper was awaiting him.

Even as he sat down to it the yacht drew out of the harbour and started on her way.

He dawdled over the food, chatting with Hendricks for the next two hours, and not until the pier at Calais was in sight, did he go on deck. His orders were of the briefest. He was to land at once and go to a certain hotel in the town, where he was to wait until morning. Then the messenger whom he was to meet, would appear, and after he had proved his identity Blake was to hand over to him the despatches he carried.

That, was all; but he knew that the despatches must be of the utmost importance when he had been chosen for the purpose and a special yacht had been placed at his service. The Fleur-de-Lys had received orders to wait at Calais until the next day and bring him back, so, bidding the captain and Hendricks au revoir until the morning, Blake landed and made his way to the hotel in question.

There he engaged a room, and, since he was tired, went upstairs at once. Before retiring, he locked the door carefully and placed his revolver under the pillow. Then he undressed, and, after smoking a final cigarette, put out the light and hopped into bed.

In less than five minutes he was asleep, his head on the pillow beneath which reposed his heavy Service-revolver and the despatches. He had been sleeping some two hours or more, and was breathing heavily, when across the room there was the faintest click, like a key being turned in a lock.

Then on the side of the room where there was a door, connecting with the adjoining room, a door silently swung back and a dark figure slipped through into Blake's room. Still he slept on, unconscious that the figure which had entered his room was now on hands and knees creeping stealthily across towards the bed.

Foot by foot the intruder drew nearer to the sleeping man, until his hand almost touched the bed. Then he turned a little in his course and made his way to the head of the bed. With infinite caution he now raised himself, and, so gently that there was scarce a sound, began to insinuate his hand beneath the pillow on which was resting Blake's head.

In the man's other hand was a large knife, which he held poised ready in case the sleeping man should awake. Inch by inch his hand went forward, until his fingers touched the butt of the revolver which lay there.

Then they came into contact with the package of despatches, but at that same moment he gave a fear-laden gasp as, through the darkness there shot a hand which gripped his throat like a vice.

A moment later Blake was off the bed, and together they went rolling about the room in a deadly struggle. Not a word did either of them speak. Nor was it necessary.

The moment the hand of the intruder had touched the pillow it had awakened Blake, and in a flash he had grasped what was happening. He also realised in the same moment why he had been chosen for what was, on the face of it, a very simple errand.

The people in London had evidently suspected that an attempt might be made to get possession of the despatches, and, in choosing Blake for the purpose, they had sent the man whom they felt confident would be best able to foil any such attempt.

It was evident to Blake in a very few moments that his antagonist was no mean one. He was as wiry as could be, and as active as a cat; and, although Blake's lightning-like move had given him a certain advantage, he had his work cut out to keep it. Over and over they rolled, sending the table crashing down as they struck it, and fetching up against the fireplace on the other side of the room.

Here an idea seemed to strike Blake's antagonist, for, with a sharp heave, he worked one arm free, and before Blake could guess his intention, had grasped the heavy iron poker from where it lay. It was so dark that Blake could not see what the other had done, and even while he was puzzling over it, and straining for a fresh hold, he felt the other's arm go back, and then something struck him full on the forehead with terrific force.

A red mist floated across his brain as the blow fell, and for a second he feared that his senses would leave him. But then came the thought of the despatches, which he must save at all costs, and with a low growl of rage he caught himself together, and hurled himself upon his antagonist with terrific force.

Before the other could stop him his fingers had closed round the poker, and he had jerked it free; then he raised it, and brought it down full in the other's face with all the strength he could muster. There was a sickening thud, a low grunt, and the man beneath him relaxed and lay quite quiescent, Blake staggered to his feet, and groped about for the switch of the light. He found it after a moment, and, pressing it down, flooded the room with light. Then he turned to regard the man who lay on the floor. He saw a crumpled heap, dressed in the uniform of a French private of the Territorials, and at first he thought he was dead.

But an examination showed that there was still life in him, though the place on his head where Blake had brought down the poker showed wickedly red in the light. It was quite evident that he would not recover for some time. So, hurriedly dressing himself, and placing the despatches in his pocket, Blake went to call the guard. He found a soldier just outside the door of the hotel, and the man, on hearing Blake's story, hurried off to fetch his captain. About a quarter of an hour later the latter came with four men, and ascended to Blake's room. The moment he saw the man on the floor he sprang back in amazement.

"Why—why," he said, in voluble French, "he is no French soldier. Him—I know him. He is German, and was in business here before the war. He left for Germany at the outbreak of hostilities, but he must have returned, unknown to the authorities."

"He must belong to a well-organised system of espionage." remarked Blake drily. "He entered this room, and attempted to get possession of something which not four people in France knew was in my possession. There is not the slightest doubt but that he knew of my arrival, and was aware of what I carried. He jolly near killed me in the dark, but I guess I gave him a fair blow myself."

"He will pay the penalty, never fear," responded the French captain grimly. "Daylight and the firing-squad will be his portion."

"He deserves it," said Blake quietly. "It is the fortune of war. If you need me as a witness, Monsieur le Capitaine I shall be pleased to attend, but I must return to England early in the morning."

"I shall take your written statement. Monsieur Blake." replied the other. "That will be sufficient from you, and then it will not be necessary to detain."

Forthwith he sat down at the table, which one of the soldiers had righted, and, drawing out a notebook and fountain-pen, began to take down the particulars which Blake gave him. Then the latter signed the statement, and, after a few more necessary details, the courteous captain and his men withdrew, taking the still unconscious spy with them.

Blake saw this time that the door connecting with the adjoining room was well barricaded, as well as the one leading to the passage; and then retiring once more, he slept soundly until morning. He was awakened by a loud knocking on his door, and, hopping out of bed, called:

"Who is it?"

"That is you, old scout, isn't it?" came back the familiar tone of a certain British staff-officer whom Blake knew intimately.

"Oh, it is you, Stafford, is it?" replied Blake. "Wait one moment until I take this barricade away from the door, and I will let you in."

"What is the matter?" asked the other, when Blake had opened the door and admitted him, a fine-looking specimen of the British officer. "Are you in a state of siege?"

"I have been for a good part of the night," replied Blake, with a smile. Then he related to the astonished officer what had happened.

"And is that how you got the beauty-spot on your forehead?" asked the latter with some concern.

Blake nodded.

"Yes. He got that one on me before I got the poker away from him and returned the compliment."

"Gad!" muttered Captain Stafford. "I don't know what can be in those despatches, but they must be jolly important. The chief told me, when he sent me to meet you, that I must get them at once on my arrival, and make the return journey during the day."

"Then I shall hand them over to you without delay," remarked Blake. "I am sorry you will not be able to stop for breakfast on the yacht with me."

"Oh, is that yours at the pier?"

"Yes—or, rather the one which was placed at my orders by the Admiralty."

"Are you taking back any despatches or anything of an important nature?" went on the captain.

"Not that I know of. I think I am travelling light. Why?"

"Because I was wondering if you would do me a favour. If you were travelling with something, I wouldn't dream of asking it. But if the yacht is just going to set you across to Dover. I am wondering if you would mind taking my sister along with you? She is a Red Cross nurse, you know, and she must go home on leave for a bit. She has been going it so hard that she has broken down, and must have a rest."

"You mean the Hon. Edwina?" asked Blake.

"Yes."

"Why, I think I met her at a dance at the Farrells'. I should be delighted to see her safely across. Where is she now?"

"Downstairs."

"Then I shall join you there as soon as I am dressed. By the way, you had better take the despatches now. I shall not be a quarter of an hour."

"Right-ho! Thanks very much! I will go down and tell my sister that you will take her across with you. She will be delighted."

He nodded, and left the room, and Blake began to dress.

A quarter of an hour later he descended to the hotel sitting room, where Captain Stafford and his sister were waiting.

The Hon. Edwina remembered Blake very well indeed and appeared quite delighted that she was going across to Dover with him.

The captain was compelled to start without delay, so Blake invited his sister to breakfast with him on the Fleur-de-Lys. So, leaving orders for her luggage to be sent on, they strolled out of the hotel and along the pier to where the yacht lay.

On the way Blake regarded his companion keenly. She was dressed in the uniform of a Red Cross nurse, and though, at first glance, she looked well enough, yet when one looked into her eyes one could see that she was on the verge of a nervous breakdown.

They chatted of trivialities as they walked along, and on reaching the yacht, Blake ordered breakfast to be served at once.

Captain Vaughan appeared as they reached the saloon, and when the introductions had been made they all sat down, including Hendricks, who appeared at the last moment.

The Hon. Edwina brightened up considerably when once the yacht pulled out and turned her nose towards Dover, and Blake, intent on keeping her entertained, led the way to the deck, where a steward had placed chairs and rugs in a sheltered spot. They were fully half-way across before he had finished telling her of recent events at home, and then he leaned back.

"Now tell me something of your life at the front," he said. "Where were you located?"

"I was in a hospital not far from Ypres," she replied. "But before I tell you of the work there, Mr. Blake, I should like to ask you a question in confidence, if I may. I have been wondering whom I could consult on a certain matter, and it seems a stroke of good fortune that I should run into you. You see, the matter about which I ask your advice is one which came under my notice while I was at the hospital, and, of course, a nurse is a good deal like a doctor. The confidences of the sick-room are sacred."

"I quite understand." answered Blake; "but if you care to honour me with your confidence, I shall, of course, respect it to the letter."

"I know you will," she murmured. "It happened this way. A few days ago there was a very severe action not far from us, and when the wounded were brought in there was one man who had done a particularly fine thing—in fact, he has been recommended for the Victoria Cross. He rescued the sergeant of his company under heavy fire, and was himself wounded badly.

"When he was brought in he was placed under my care, and he was quite delirious. He seemed to be fearfully unhappy over something, for he kept talking continually of something which he referred to as being too late to mend.

"I tried to soothe him, but he grew steadily worse, and finally began begging me to let him die. Now, when he was brought in his name was given, but in his delirium he talked of himself as an entirely different individual, so I could only come to the conclusion that he had enlisted under an assumed name.

"The name he kept using in his delirium is one which seemed to sound familiar to me, though I can't seem to place it. And that is where I am wondering if you can help me. You see, I don't know London very well, since we rarely come up to town, and, of course, I am ignorant of a good deal that goes on there. But I thought if there was anything in my mind which I had failed to recall, you might be able to tell me what it was."

"I shall be glad to do whatever I can," replied Blake earnestly. "What is the name?"

"The name is Fenmore. I am certain I have— Why, what is the matter?"

She broke off, and asked the question as Blake turned sharply towards her with a startled exclamation.

"Did I understand you to say that the name was Fenmore?" he asked evenly.

"Yes."

"Do you by any chance know the first name?

"No; but perhaps it is the same as he used in his assumed name."

"What was that?"

"Robert."

"Ah! I think I can tell you a good deal that you would like to know," said Blake, after a slight pause. "As a matter of fact, you have put me on the track of a man whom I am most anxious to find; that is if he is the one whom you seem to think he is. Don't you remember reading in the papers some few months ago about the sudden disappearance of a certain Robert Fenmore? He gained some notoriety at the time through his gambling proclivities."

She sat up suddenly.

"I knew the name was familiar to me. I remember it all now. He disappeared, leaving a wife, didn't he?"

"Yes."

"I remember—I remember. Tell me, Mr. Blake, why are you seeking him? Did he do anything wrong?"

"No, not exactly, and I am sorry that I am not at liberty to tell you why I am seeking him; though I assure you, there is no danger for him in my search. I wish to find him for his own good."

"If he did anything wrong he certainly has made up for it," she murmured softly. "They say his deed was a magnificent one."

"I have always thought that Bob Fenmore was a good deal of a man," responded Blake. "I shall go to him as quickly as possible, and take him some good news. Much has happened since he went away, and I think he has learned his lesson."

"When a man gets into the firing-line all his old weaknesses seem to be miserable and mean," she said. "Fenmore is every inch a man now."

Blake nodded.

"I hope so. Later on I shall be free to tell you the whole story, and then you will understand why I want to find him. But why did you seek my advice in this matter, Miss Stafford?"

"Because, Mr. Blake, I could not help but sympathise with the man. It seemed to me that if he had done anything wrong he had more than made reparation, and I thought while I was in England I would see if there was something I could do in the matter. If I could help him in any way to make a fresh start I should like to do so."

"I quite understand how you feel," responded Blake. "And I think, from what you have told me, I shall be able to take steps which will help him as you wish him to be helped. At any rate, if you will give me the name under which he is now known, and the name of the hospital where he is at present, I will do what I can, and keep you advised. Before long I hope it will be my pleasure to send you good news."

And so before the Fleur-de-Lys reached Dover Blake was in possession of all she knew about the man who had done such a fine deed on the battlefield, and who was known as Private Fraser. But as they entered the train, and were borne speeding towards London, Blake little dreamed of the stirring events which had taken place during his absence.

PRIVATE FRASER'S PLUCKY RESCUE ON THE FIELD OF BATTLE.

Fraser was deaf to all, and obsessed by only one idea—to make the trench with his sergeant. He was drawing very near, and as his comrades saw the look of agonised determination on his face, half a dozen of them leaped up, and rushed forward.

The Sixth Chapter.   Plans Which Miscarried.

YVONNE was able to get away from the Fenmore flat a little before eleven on the evening which Blake went to the Continent. She had spent most of the time with Marion Fenmore soothing and comforting her and witnessing the young mother's delight in the baby which had come into her life after so much suffering and unhappiness.

About half-past ten Marion had dropped off into a peaceful sleep, and Yvonne whispering to the nurse that she was going out, and might not be back until very late if at all, donned her things, and taking a leash from the hall, fastened it to the truant Pedro's collar. As for that sagacious canine he had the time of his life.

What had possessed him to follow Yvonne home it is impossible to say. He had always had a tremendous liking for her, and even when it had been Blake's duty to track her down he had had little assistance from Pedro for instead of regarding her as an enemy, he had always been only too ready to submit to her caresses. As Tinker had put it more than once, he was a very discerning fellow.

But whatever his reason for doing so, he had followed her that afternoon, and had calmly ensconced himself on the steps until she had happened to open the door. And as Yvonne had said, he had shown a decided partiality for chocolate creams with which she had stuffed him, until she became alarmed at the extraordinary capacity he showed for disposing of them.

He had been quite content to stretch out in the study during the evening, but when Yvonne got ready to go out, he was on hand waiting.

He submitted quietly to the leash, and when they emerged from the flat started off towards Baker Street, as though fully aware that it was to be their destination. But Yvonne had no intention of walking, so, standing on the kerb, she kept tight hold of the leash while she hailed a taxi.

Then, pushing the big fellow in, she gave the address, and entered herself. On arriving at Baker Street she dismissed the cab, and mounted the steps. In answer to her ring Mrs. Bardell came to the door, and in response to Yvonne's question said:

"No, miss, Tinker is not in. But will you come in and wait? Before Mr. Blake went away, he said if you should come, and Tinker had not returned, you were to wait if you wished."

Yvonne thanked her, and entered. Mrs. Bardell led the way along to the consulting-room where a cheerful fire was burning, and before departing drew up the easy-chair for Yvonne's convenience. Then she left her alone, and, throwing off her furs, Yvonne sat down, while Pedro stretched out on the rug at her feet. It was only natural that, being in Blake's home, she should feel the memories of the past surging up.

When she came at other times either Blake or Tinker was there, and her visit was more of a formal affair. But now she was there alone, waiting almost as though it were her home, too. She blushed softly as the thought came to her, and had Blake seen her at that moment, lying back in the big chair, and looking delightfully winsome, it is difficult to say what feelings might have assailed him as well.

Of late Yvonne had been a complete enigma to him. In the old days, when her girlish heart had been given to him, her love had shone forth from her misty eyes whenever in his presence.

But ever since she had written him from the old place in Surrey, telling him of her determination to seek the excitement of the old life, her demeanour towards him had changed.

She had been perfectly friendly, and since the outbreak of war had assisted him more than once in his work, but not even a momentary flash of the old expression did he catch, and, manlike, he felt that there was something missing.

For the first time in his life he found himself wondering about the existence of another man. Had she met someone whom she could like sufficiently to encourage? As he asked himself this question, Blake felt a most unaccountable savageness towards the possible unknown, and unconsciously his hands would clench fiercely.

Then he would remind himself that when he could have had her love he had refused it, and that he had no right to feel any regret if she should choose someone else.

In other words, Sexton Blake, the man who was such a master at analysing other people's minds and motives, failed utterly to understand himself when a mere slip of a girl puzzled him. And had anyone suggested that for the first time in his life he was experiencing the pangs of jealousy, he would have scouted the idea savagely. But, as a matter of fact, that is exactly what he was feeling, and yet had he but known it, Yvonne felt for him what she had always felt. Nothing would change her in that way, and no other interest would ever enter into the corner of her heart which was dedicated to Blake. She might marry in the future—who could tell? and she would give to her husband love and respect. But nothing would ever touch the rose-leaves of memory which lay in her heart. She had simply locked away that part of the past, and her own fingers would never hold the key which would unlock it.

If Blake ever wished to see it again it must be his own volition which would release the little door which had been closed upon it.

Yvonne had been sitting there dreaming for some time when she was brought back to the present by a low growl from Pedro. The big fellow had come to his feet with a bound, and was standing rigidly, listening, his muzzle pointed towards the door which opened into the passage which led to the laboratory.

Yvonne bent forward, and, catching Pedro's collar, listened too. At first she could hear nothing; but after a moment a soft creaking noise came from somewhere beyond the door and she barely succeeded in placing a cautioning hand over Pedro's muzzle before he growled again.

Softly she rose and, tiptoeing towards the door, pressed her ear against it. Now she could distinctly hear the sound of movements in the direction of the laboratory, and even as she stood there she heard a door open, and was certain she could make out the stealthy footsteps of someone coming down the passage.

Like a flash she sprang back, and, catching Pedro's collar again, dragged him towards the dressing-room, drawing her revolver as she went. She was positive that whoever had gained access to the house had no business there, for Pedro was so distinctly hostile. He went with her reluctantly, but evidently trusted her completely, for he was docile enough when she whispered to him.

She reckoned that the intruder must have come in by the laboratory window; but what his purpose might be she couldn't guess. But it was in order to find out that purpose that she was attempting to conceal herself.

When she reached the dressing-room she saw a large cupboard, and towards this she went. Opening the door, she saw that it was full of clothes; and she had scarcely squeezed in, dragging the dog after her, when she heard the door of the consulting-room open, and could distinguish a stealthy step.

It stopped just then, and for a few moments there was dead silence. Evidently the intruder was taking note of his surroundings. Then suddenly it could be heard again coming straight towards the door of the dressing-room. Yvonne held her breath and waited.

It was necessary to place her hand firmly on Pedro's muzzle, for he was growing restless. But Yvonne wished, if possible, to find out the purpose of the intruder before making a move.

On he came until he had pushed open the door of the dressing-room and entered. Then he paused at the door for a moment before advancing; and, peeping forth from her place of concealment, Yvonne could see that he carried an electric pocket-torch, with which he was examining his surroundings.

Then he advanced; and she heard him go into the bed-room. Now she pushed open the door ever so cautiously, and, still retaining her hold on Pedro's collar, stole across the room until she stood beside the electric light switch. Thus she waited for the reappearance of the other; and Pedro, seeming to sense that she had some definite plan, waited beside her.

Five minutes passed, during which Yvonne could hear the man moving about in the bed-room; then the door opened suddenly, and he came out.

At the very moment his foot came over the threshold Yvonne pressed the switch, flooding the room with light. There was a startled gasp and an oath from the man as he sprang back in consternation, and while he stood poised, as though debating what to do, Yvonne saw that he was a burly fellow, with a lowering brow and a great, jagged scar running down one side of his face.

Had Tinker been there he could have told her that he answered to the name of Max, and that for some time past he had acted as servant to the man who had been murdered the previous evening. But Tinker at that moment was in dire peril, and, of course Yvonne had no idea of the man's identity, or of his purpose in being there. But that did not deter her from taking matters into her own hands, and, as he hesitated, gazing into the muzzle of the revolver which she held without a tremor, she said coolly:

"Well, my friend, and what do you want in here?"

The man glared at her for a moment; but it was evident that he was not much intimidated by the weapon. No doubt he took Yvonne for some girl living in the house, and imagined that the revolver was a piece of bluff on her part. He did not dream for a moment that he was facing Mademoiselle Yvonne, whose finished methods of outwitting the law were as far superior to the raw attempts of Johann Mulberg and Marion Paul as science is ahead of blind imagining.

Had he known that, he might have considered for a moment before he did what he did do. As he heard her question his lip curled, and, without deigning to reply, he made a rush for the door.

At the moment he started Yvonne pulled the trigger, and the bullet sped straight for the spot at which she had aimed— the shoulder. The same instant saw Pedro break free and leap for the man's throat, and they both went down with a terrific crash.

Yvonne, seeing the great fellow's foaming muzzle at the man's throat, and realising how quickly Pedro would tear his throat out once his teeth came together, rushed towards them and grasped the dog by the collar. He worried away at his victim, disregarding her entreaties for a little; but finally he yielded, and backed away a few steps. Ordering Pedro to watch the man, she turned to him.

"You made a bad mistake then, my friend," she said evenly. "I gave you fair warning before I fired, but you evidently thought I didn't mean it. Now, I am going to leave the dog to guard you while I find something with which to bind you, and if you value your life I should advise you to rest quietly. If you make a move I shouldn't care to answer for the consequences."

The man glared at her sullenly, but made no reply; and Yvonne, trusting to Pedro to look after the prisoner, made her way back to the consulting-room, where she had noticed a lariat hanging on the wall. This she took down, and, returning to the dressing-room, soon had the captive trussed up securely.

She searched round until she found something which was suitable for a gag; and when she had finished the prisoner was secure for the time at least.

She stood thinking for a few minutes, trying to decide what to do with him, and then she decided to wait until she had seen Tinker.

So, bending down, she grasped the man under the shoulders, and, half dragging, half carrying him, she made her way to the bed-room. Here she let him sink to the floor, and went out, closing the door; but had the room not been dark she would have seen in the man's eyes a look of the most awful terror which ever rested in human orbs.

But Yvonne did not see this, and, being quite unaware of it, went back to the consulting-room. She seated herself at the desk, and, leaning her chin on her hand, tried to puzzle out the occurrence which had just taken place.

"He had some distinct purpose in going into the bedroom," she murmured, after a bit. "He was no ordinary burglar. If he had been he would have examined things out here. Now, I wonder if his visit here has any bearing on the case which is occupying Mr. Blake and Tinker? If so, it may also have something to do with Tinker's movements to-day. And, by the same token, he ought to be here by now. I wonder what I had better do? I don't like to go about the flat investigating things, and there is no use in sending for Mrs. Bardell. She wouldn't know what to do. I wonder how he got in, anyway? I suppose by way of the laboratory window. Perhaps he has an accomplice outside. I'll just go and have a look, anyway."

Suiting the action to the word, Yvonne rose, and, opening the door leading to the passage, went along to the laboratory.

The place was in darkness, but against the sky outside she could make out the shape of the window. From where she stood it was easy to see that it was wide open. There was no doubt now by which way the intruder had come.

Yvonne walked across, and was in the act of closing it when, happening to glance out, she saw a pair of lights in the lane at the rear. Intuition told her that it was a motor of some sort, and that it was by this the man had come. It must be still waiting for him.

As she realised this a daring plan came to Yvonne, and she acted on it at once. Hurrying back to the consulting-room, she wrote a hurried note to Tinker, telling him she had called, and would return. She also told him of the prisoner in the bed-room, and described briefly how she had caught him. She propped the note against the inkstand on the desk, and put on her furs; then, slipping the leash on Pedro, she returned to the laboratory.

It was comparatively easy work getting through the window, but she noticed that when she reached the ground outside she could no longer see the lights of the motor. She concluded this must be on account of the fence, and a moment later, when she reached that obstruction, saw that her surmise was correct. It was not so easy getting over the fence into the lane, but at last she managed it, dragging Pedro after her.

Now she could see the twin lights of the car just ahead of her; and when she had drawn still closer to it saw that it was not a private motor, as she had feared, but a taxi. The next thing to discover was if there was anybody in it besides the driver.

The latter, evidently, had caught sight of her figure, for as she approached he descended. But when he saw that it was a woman, and not the man whom he was expecting, he started back in surprise.

Taking advantage of his momentary confusion, Yvonne went close to the window and peered inside. A feeling of relief went through her as she saw that the interior was empty. Then she turned to the driver.

"The fare you brought is not returning now," she said coolly. "I am going back in his stead. I want you to drive me back to just where you picked him up."

"You mean up the lane?" he asked gruffly.

Yvonne had no idea what he meant, but answered readily: "Yes, to the exact spot."

"All right; get in," he replied.

She opened the door, and waited until Pedro had got in; then she entered herself, and a moment later the cab began to back up. When the driver had succeeded in turning, he drove round into Baker Street, and from there went by several turnings along to Hyde Park Corner. From there he drove on to Knightsbridge, and suddenly, as he made a sharp turn to the right, Yvonne saw, with surprise, that they were close to the small hotel where she had been only the night before, when in pursuit of the Fenmore necklace.

Now she began to give her attention to the affair in earnest, and when the cab turned up the narrow lane behind the hotel, and drew up at the very spot where she had climbed the fence the night before, she was not surprised. It began to look as if she had stumbled upon something worth while. As soon as the taxi stopped she opened the door and descended; then she turned to the driver.

"Look here, I will give you an extra sovereign over your fare if you will do as I want you to."

"What is it, miss?"

"I want you to drive farther, up the lane, and stop in the shadow where you can't be seen. Then I want you to put out all your lights, and wait for me until I return. You will also have to be careful about smoking, in case you are seen. Will you do this?"

"I'm always open to make money, miss," he said briefly. "Watch from here, and you can judge if I go up far enough."

She stood and waited while he drove on up the lane a little; then he stopped the cab, and extinguished the lamps. He had chosen a perfect spot for the purpose, for, try as she would, Yvonne could not distinguish the lines of the taxi after he had put out the lights. She ran along to him, and told him the position would do; then she returned to the rear of the hotel, and proceeded to get over the fence.

At last she managed to get herself and Pedro over, and had she been in doubt which way to go, the big fellow settled it in making straight for the outbuilding by way of which she had entered the flat the previous night. She wondered if it were the trail of the man she had captured which he was following, and decided that it must be, though there was a possibility that it might be Tinker's.

Never for a moment did she guess what had happened to Tinker in that flat only a little while before, and much less did she dream of the terrible peril in which he was at that very moment.

She sought about until she found the same foothold which had served her before; then she swung herself to the roof, and pulled on the leash, while Pedro sprang after her. Then, laying a cautioning hand on his muzzle, she began to creep up the sloping surface towards the kitchen window. She could see that the room had a light in it, and as she drew still nearer she could make out a narrow slit between the sill and the lower sash.

Already it had been obvious to her that the man she had caught at Baker Street had come from Marion Paul's flat, and now it was evident that he had left by way of the kitchen window, neglecting to close it tightly after him. She crept on still further, until by raising herself on her knees she could see the interior of the kitchen. And as she did so a wave of horror went over her at what she saw.

Inside the room were three people—two women and a man. One of the women she recognised as Marion Paul, and the other she took from her dress to be a maid. The man was short and stout, and wore large spectacles of a bluish tinge. She saw at first glance that he was of Teutonic descent.

But that was not all she saw. Lying on the floor, bound and gagged and, as far as she could see, unconscious, was Tinker. He was the object of the attention of the other three, for while the two women looked on, the man pointed to the lad, and gesticulated excitedly. Through the narrow opening at the bottom of the sash Yvonne could hear perfectly, and, with a thrill of horror, she realised that the man was calmly proposing Tinker's death.

"I tell you it is the only thing to do," he was saying. "You have nothing to fear. I will do everything, and get rid of the body afterwards. He must have overheard every word we said, and if we let him go we will only be running our heads into a noose. You take Zela inside with you Marion, and wait there. It will be all over in a few minutes!"

As he spoke he pointed to a glass bottle which stood on the table, and to which was fitted a rubber bulb and syringe. It appeared to be half full of a colourless liquid which looked exactly like water, but which, was evidently of the most potent nature from the way he referred to it.

"Just a little spraying of that," he said, "and he will never wake. Now go along, the pair of you, and I will settle him in no time!"

In obedience to his orders the two women turned and left the room.

No sooner had they gone than the man picked up the bottle, and, taking the bulb in his hand, bent over the lad. Now it flashed upon Yvonne what his purpose was. The colourless liquid in the bottle was a strong poison, to inhale which meant certain death. And this was what was intended for Tinker.

She grasped her revolver, bringing it steadily into position. If the man bent another inch in Tinker's direction she would pull the trigger. But suddenly something seemed to occur to him, and he laid the bottle back, muttering as he did so:

"I had better send Zela out for a taxi, and arrange for it to come round to the back. Then there will be no delay. If I take Zela with me, we can support the body between us, and the driver won't suspect anything. We can drop him out on the road, and get back to town. Yes, that is the best plan."

He turned now, and, opening the door, left the room. The door sagged forward a little, shutting off Yvonne's view of the hall, and in the same moment a plan came to her. Could she carry it through? She would try.

Ordering Pedro to lie down, she softly raised the window, and climbed over the sill into the room. For a brief moment the idea occurred to her to unbind Tinker, and take him with her. But she realised that the man might return at any moment, and, not only were the bonds tight, but the lad was unconscious, and it would be impossible for her to carry him alone.

But there was still something she could do, so, springing across to the table, she jerked the bulb off the bottle, and, holding it at arm's length, poured the contents down the sink. Then she turned on the tap a little, and let as much water run into the bottle as there had been of the other liquid. Then she fixed on the bulb, and laid the bottle back on the table.

A noise up the hall caused her to spring back towards the window, and she had just managed to climb out and close it after her when the bespectacled individual re-entered the room.

He walked over to a towel-rack, and, taking a towel from it, wrapped it over his mouth and nose. Then he went to the table, and took up the bottle again. Holding it up, he shook it slightly, and as she saw his lips part in an evil smile Yvonne knew that he did not suspect for a moment that the contents had been changed since he had been out of the room.

Holding it close to Tinker's face, he pressed the bulb several times, spraying the contents all over the lad's face, but concentrating most of his attention in the region of the mouth and nose. When he felt satisfied that sufficient had been applied, he put the bottle on the table and stood back.

"In an hour he will be as dead as a log," he said aloud; and for the first time in her life Yvonne realised that she had witnessed a thing that, but for her interference, would have been cold, deliberate murder. And in the same moment something seemed to whisper to her that before her stood the man who had murdered Harold Craig.

Then the man unwrapped the towel from his face, and as the sound of a taxi came to Yvonne's ears she slipped back down the roof, and dropped lightly to the ground. Scurrying across to the rear wall, she got over somehow, and dragged Pedro after her as she raced up the lane towards her own cab. She had barely succeeded in reaching it when another taxi turned into the lane, and stopped at the rear of the hotel.

"That is no doubt the one for which Mr. Murderer sent," she muttered as she watched it.

A few minutes passed before anything else occurred, and then she saw a black, moving blotch issue from the yard of the hotel, and knew it must be the man and the maid, supporting the supposed dying body of Tinker. She saw them enter the cab, and heard the door slam. Then the taxi began to back out of the lane, and as it did so Yvonne leaned towards her own driver.

"You see that cab?" she said quickly.

"Yes, miss."

"Another sovereign still if you follow it and do not lose it. But for goodness' sake be careful that they don't see you!"

With a nod the man was in the seat, and a second later was turning to start in pursuit. He took the corner into Knightsbridge on two wheels, and far up the thoroughfare, heading towards Hyde Park Corner, was the quarry.

The chase led straight through to the Corner, and from there went along Park Lane to Connaught Place. Now the leading taxi turned down the Edgware Road, and kept on as fast as the driver dared to. Yvonne's driver was on its tail all the time, and they went dashing ahead for the best part of an hour until the open country showed.

As they tore along through the night Yvonne puzzled over the daring of the people ahead in taking a taxi for their purpose. Then it occurred to her that the driver was probably but one of the gang, and, as a matter of fact, this was the case.

They had reached a long, steep hill, and were going slowly up it, when suddenly Yvonne's driver put on the brake, and drew up with a sharp jerk. In a moment Yvonne had the door open, and was out on the road.

She was turning to ask the reason for the stop, when over in the gutter she saw a dark bundle. Instinctively she knew what she would find there. Hurrying across to it, she bent down, and in the faint light saw the still form of Tinker.

In a few minutes the driver had joined her, and together they lifted him up. Yvonne noticed as they carried him across to the taxi, that all his bonds had been removed, and concluded that this had been done before he had been hurled bodily from the other taxi on its way up the hill. The moment he had been laid inside, she turned to the driver, and together they glanced up the hill. The rear light of the other cab was just disappearing over the brow.

"I will look after this lad," said Yvonne quickly. "Go after that, other. If you succeed in following it back, your reward will be enough to repay you."

"You leave it to me, miss," he answered. "I'll catch them up, or my name is mud."

With that he leaped for the seat, and Yvonne jumped into the cab. While they groaned up the hill, she bent over Tinker, and felt his pulse. She found, with a thrill of satisfaction that it was beating regularly. Now she reached for her hag, and after fumbling about amongst the contents for a bit, drew out a small bottle of ammonia. This she applied cautiously to the lad's nostrils, and after a few minutes, had the satisfaction of seeing him open his eyes. He stirred uneasily and sat up.

"Where am I? What has happened?" he asked drowsily.

"It is all right, Tinker," answered Yvonne, as she applied the bottle once again.

This time the powerful fumes brought him up sitting, and he gazed in amazement at his surroundings.

"You, Mademoiselle Yvonne?" he gasped. "Where did you come from, and what am I doing in a motor? Where— what— Oh, by thunder! I remember that I was in the flat and had a fight, but that is the last."

"Listen, Tinker," said Yvonne, "and I will explain as much as I know."

So she told him how she had gone to the small hotel where Marion Paul had her flat, and how through the kitchen window she had seen him lying bound and gagged on the floor. Then she explained how she had defeated the murderous plan which had been made against him, winding up with a description of the chase into the country.

"It is quite evident that they think you are certain to succumb to the effects of the poison they think they administered to you," she went on, "That was why they undid your bonds and threw you out of the cab on the way up the hill. They were sure that you would be dead by the time you were discovered. What our bespectacled friend would say if he knew that he had methodically sprayed your face with harmless water instead of deadly poison it is difficult to imagine. I don't think he will find one language sufficient in which to express himself. Now tell me what really happened at the flat, Tinker."

The lad, who was feeling much better by now, first took Yvonne's hand, and thanked her huskily for what she had done.

"You make little of it," he said, "but I know how much nerve it took to get into that kitchen when the man was expected back at any moment, and to empty the poison from the bottle. It was magnificent, and the guv'nor will think so, too, when I tell him."

"You must not do that, Tinker," she protested, flushing in the dark. "I would rather you let it drop. If I was able to help you, you know I was glad to do so. Both you and Mr. Blake have done much for me in the past."

"I shall tell him just the same," responded Tinker firmly. "If it hadn't been for what you did, I should have been lying back there in the gutter dead. Now I shall tell you what happened to me."

He began with his arrival on the scene earlier in the day, and related to Yvonne all that had occurred to him until he had been discovered in the flat by the Pekingese, and described as much as he remembered of the fight which followed.

"That is all I can tell you," he said, as he finished. "One of them, the man with the glasses, I think, got a handkerchief over my face, and that was the end of me. It was saturated with chloroform. But, by jingo, mademoiselle, I overheard enough there to prove that the whole four of them had a hand in the murder of Craig. They are a daring gang, and the old fellow with the glasses seems to be the head of it."

"I agree with you," she said. "In my opinion he is the one who actually carried out the murder of Craig. But we shall submit the evidence we have gathered to Mr. Blake when he returns, and see what he thinks of it."

"I think he already suspects Marion Paul of having something to do with it," remarked Tinker. "He was very keen that I should not lose sight of her."

"At any rate, both she and the maid countenanced the killing of you," said Yvonne. "And now let me see how the chase is progressing. This road by which we are returning turns so frequently it is almost impossible to tell whether we are keeping the other taxi in sight or not."

Even as she spoke, they turned into a stretch of straight road and about three hundred yards ahead could be seen the tail-light of the other car. From the way it was rocking, it was evident to them that it had grown suspicious of them, and was endeavouring to shake them off. But Yvonne's driver stuck to it grimly, and so far was holding his own. On they raced in this fashion for another two or three miles, until they reached a long hill down which they raced at top speed. The front taxi was going in the most reckless fashion now, and if they came to a sharp turning in the road, it would need all the driver's finesse to negotiate it safely. Tinker and Yvonne were bending forward tensely watching the chase, when suddenly the lad uttered a low exclamation.

"By thunder, I know this hill, mademoiselle! Look at that train over to the left of the valley. It crosses the road at the bottom by a level crossing. It is one of the most dangerous places in the country. We had better warn our driver to watch out for it!"

Yvonne nodded, and thrusting her head out of the window, told the man what Tinker had said.

"It is all right, miss," he replied. "I have control of the car, and will go slowly when I get to the bottom."

Yvonne withdrew her head, and again watched their progress. A moment later, they made a turning which brought them in sight of the bottom, and just as they did so, the brilliant headlight of a train swept round a curve and sped towards the crossing. In its glare, they could see the other taxi racing for the crossing in an endeavour to make it before the train reached it.

While it was still some distance away, the whistle of the locomotive shrieked warningly, but the taxi kept on. The driver was evidently sure that he could make it. Yvonne's driver applied the brakes, and they began to slow up, and so, as they came to a stop about thirty yards from the crossing, they watched with dilated eyes that mad race ahead.

There was another shriek of the engine's whistle, then the taxi reached the crossing. Would it get across? The headlight of the engine was now perilously close, and was sweeping onwards like the blazing eye of some giant monster.

Then the cab seemed to hover for a moment on the rails, and the next instant the iron monster was upon it. There was a terrific crashing, rending sound, a faint cry which was immediately lost in the greater roar, a momentary vision of the cab being hurled skywards, then the train thundered on with shrieking brakes to come to a standstill some distance away.

Yvonne shivered, and turned to Tinker.

"Oh, it was awful!" she gasped.

He nodded briefly.

"It is impossible that they could have escaped," he replied. "The engine seemed to drop right on them. There are people from the train coming down the track. Let us drive on and see what has happened."

They went ahead slowly until they had drawn near the shattered remains of the taxi, and leaving Yvonne, where she was, Tinker jumped out and went forward. He arrived at the spot just as a couple of train officials ran up.

"Did you see it?" asked the guard hurriedly.

Tinker nodded.

"Yes; all of it! I suppose you want me for a witness?"

"Yes; and your driver."

"All right, we will give you our names. But it wasn't the fault of the engine-driver."

"But where are the remains of the people who were in the cab. Have you any idea how many there were?"

"I have reason to believe that there was a man and a woman besides the driver," replied Tinker slowly.

Now one of the other members of the train's crew came running up, and whispered that they had found the remains of a woman and a man, and shortly after another reported that he had come upon the driver, dead and terribly mutilated.

All three must have been killed instantly, but, shocking as was the tragedy, Tinker could not help but think that they had received only a sudden retribution for their deeds. He kept this opinion to himself though, and merely gave his name and address. Then he called the driver of his own taxi, who gave his, and neither of them mentioned Yvonne's presence in the cab. Then the crew of the train carried the remains to the guard's van, and the train went on.

Tinker and Yvonne, much sobered by the sudden tragedy drove straight to Baker Street, scarcely speaking on the way and at the lad's earnest request she came in for a little in order to discuss at length the next move they should make in case Blake should remain on the Continent for some days.

When they entered the consulting-room, Tinker went to the mantel, and from the interior of the idol took the letter he knew must be there. He read it at once, and when he finished, turned to Yvonne with a smile.

"The guv'nor suspects Marion Paul all right," he said. "I can tell from this. He urges me not to lose track of her for a moment. Now will you sit down mademoiselle, and we can talk over things."

"Oh, by the way, Tinker," she said suddenly, "I was nearly

forgetting the prisoner in the bed-room. Hadn't we better see how he is?"

"By jingo, yes!" he replied. "I had forgotten him, too! You wait here, and I will see to him!"

As he spoke Tinker opened the door of the dressing-room and started through towards the bed-room. Just as his fingers were on the handle of the door he noticed a strong, pungent odour which seemed to pervade the place.

"I say, mademoiselle," he called, "just step in here for a moment, will you?"

She came a moment later and stood beside him.

"Isn't that a peculiar smell?" he asked. "What do you suppose it is? I can't place it at all."

For a moment Yvonne stood sniffing, then suddenly she turned to him.

"I knew there was something familiar in that odour," she said. "It is the same smell which that liquid had which the man in the flat was going to spray on your face. It is the smell of the poison!"

"But where on earth is it coming from?" he said in puzzlement. "How would it get here?"

"Open the door, Tinker," said Yvonne quickly. "I am beginning to understand, I think, why the man Pedro and I caught should come into the bed-room."

The lad turned the handle and opened the door. Then he sprang back sharply.

"Steady!" he cried. "The room is full of the stuff. Stay here until I get the window open!"

Ducking his head, he dashed through the bed-room and jerked up the sash, then he raced back, and, going to the consulting-room, opened the window there in order to cause a draught through.

Returning to the door of the bed room, he saw that Yvonne was peering in at a bundle on the floor.

"There he is!" she whispered. "Do you suppose the poison has taken effect on him?"

"We shall soon see," replied Tinker grimly. "I am going to drag him out and have a look at him."

So saying, he dashed once more into the room, and, catching the prostrate man by the shoulders, dragged him into the dressing-room. Yvonne switched on the light, and they both turned to look at him. In a single glance they saw that he was past all they could do for him. His face was swollen and black, and his hands clenched convulsively. The great scar on his cheek showed livid against the deeper colour, and as he saw it, Tinker gave a gasp of amazement.

"Why, it is the man who was at the flat," he said quickly. "If it hadn't been for him I might have escaped. He must have left soon after, and come on here. Oh, by jingo, I have it now, mademoiselle. I remember that they had a long whispered conversation regarding the guv'nor just before I was discovered, and I knew it was something they intended to do to him, though I couldn't catch what was said. But don't you see now what it was? They planned to kill him. This man was to come on here and place some of the poison in the bed-room, so that when the guv'nor retired he would be overcome. They took a chance of not finding him here. Of course, they did not know that he had gone away, and never dreamed you would be here."

"I believe you are right," answered Yvonne. "When he came in he went straight to the bed-room as soon as he located it. That must have been his purpose. Of course, I didn't know he was one of that gang, or I might have guessed something of his purpose. Still, even though he came with the intention of encompassing Mr. Blake's death, I'm sorry I dragged him back into the bed-room and left him there!"

"I shouldn't worry about that," responded Tinker. "You didn't know that he had saturated the place with poison, he only got what he intended the guv'nor should get. By jingo, mademoiselle, it is jolly queer I think! Look what happened to those in the taxi, and now look at this. I tell you there is something more than accident in it, mademoiselle."

"I believe you are right, Tinker," she said softly. "In their case, at least, Fate has been swift and sure. But there is still one remaining— Marion Paul."

"Yes, and we must keep from her the knowledge of what has happened. The papers will be full of the accident on the crossing to-night, but perhaps the guv'nor will be home before she hears of it, or identifies the victims as her friends. I suppose I might as well take the gag out of this fellow's mouth and untie his bonds. Then I can take him to the laboratory and leave him there until morning."

Suiting the action to the word, he did as he had suggested, and when he had placed the body of the man in the laboratory, he closed the door and returned to the consulting-room, murmuring as he went:

"Hoist by his own petard if ever a man was."

Then he and Yvonne seated themselves and went carefully over all the evidence they had gathered. And not until the first streaks of dawn were showing in the east did they rise. Then they had made their plans for the coming day, and since neither of them felt like sleep, they issued forth from the house and made their way Citywards in order to get breakfast, for neither of them felt like eating while that still figure lay in the laboratory.

Tinker and Yvonne breakfasted leisurely, and it was past eight o'clock when they finished. They returned together to Baker Street in order to see if there was any word from Blake, and on arriving there found a wire which had been sent from Calais saying that he would arrive at Charing Cross about half-past ten.

There were two other cablegrams addressed to Blake, but since his master would arrive so soon Tinker left them unopened. Then they made their plans as agreed on the night before. While Yvonne went to Knightsbridge and endeavoured to get into Marion Paul's flat Tinker was to go to the station, meet Blake, tell him all that had occurred, and bring him on at once to Knightsbridge after he had decided whether to ask Inspector Thomas to come or not.

Yvonne hailed a taxi outside the door, and, telling the man where to drive, leaned back and examined her revolver. Then she thrust it where she could get at it in case of need, and closed her eyes until the cab drew up in front of the hotel.

She dismissed it there, and, entering, went straight to the lift. The boy took her up without question and pointed out to her the door of Marion Paul's flat. She approached it with a strange little flutter, for if her calculations were correct she would find Marion Paul there alone, and no doubt a good deal puzzled at the non-appearance of the others who had left, on such sinister errands the night before.

Yvonne pressed the bell, and heard it ring in the distance, then, after a few moments, a step sounded inside, and the door was opened. She saw at once that it was Marion Paul herself, and though Yvonne had little love for her after witnessing the suffering of Marion Fenmore, she was shocked, and felt a throb of pity for the woman. Her appearance was ghastly.

She was still in the blue house gown which she had worn the previous night, and it was evident from the haggard expression of her face that she had not been to bed.

Her eyes widened with sudden apprehension as she saw that the early caller was a total stranger, and she made a motion as though to close the door. But Yvonne had anticipated this, and deftly slipped inside before it could be done.

"Who are you?" asked Marion Paul, endeavouring to speak curtly.

"I shall tell you when we are inside." replied Yvonne coolly. "I wish to have a conversation with you, Miss Paul."

"But I don't know you!" snapped the other. "What possible reason can you have for visiting me at this time of the day?"

"I think it would be best for you to grant me an interview without delay," responded Yvonne, with meaning in her tone, and the other, yielding she knew not why, led the way to the study.

She seated herself at the table, and Yvonne, choosing a chair near the door, looked Marion Paul in the eyes.

"You do not know me?" she asked.

The actress shook her head.

"No; I don't think I have ever seen you before."

"Then permit me to introduce myself," went on Yvonne. "I am Mademoiselle Yvonne Cartier."

"Ah!" The exclamation broke from Marion Paul as she heard Yvonne's name, and a sudden gleam of fear came into her eyes. "I have heard of you," she said slowly. "Why do you come here? What do you want of me?"

"I have many reasons for coming," replied Yvonne. "But first of all I want to tell you that it was I who took the Fenmore necklace from the safe in your sitting-room." She held up her hand as the other made to speak. "Wait! Let me finish! I did not take it, as you may think, in order to profit by it. You may have heard a good deal about and are apt to draw that conclusion. I took it from you order to return it to the woman to whom it belonged— Fenmore. It was never intended for you, and you know it."

"How do you know that?" whispered the other.

"Because I have read the letter which Bob Fenmore was supposed to have written to you when he sent it, and I know that it was never worded by him with the intention that you should read it. That letter was meant for his wife and since he gave the necklace to the one for whom the letter was intended, therefore it was meant for her."

"But the letter and necklace were both sent to me," put in Marion Paul curtly.

"Perhaps —through Harold Craig." said Yvonne coolly "There is no use in keeping up that bluff any longer. One of the keenest minds in existence has read the riddle of that letter, and I agree with him, though I did not know anything about the letter when I took the necklace from the safe. I simply watched my opportunity and got possession of it because Marion Fenmore has suffered so. And a good deal of it has been through you Marion Paul.

"Now, I shall go on to the next thing which is included in my reason for coming," went on Yvonne. "I want to tell you that I know all about what went on in this flat last night."

"What do you mean?"

"I mean, I know about the lad who gained access here, and I know about the methods which were taken to get rid of him. When the man with the glasses stood out in the kitchen here, and prepared to spray that helpless lad's face with a deadly poison, he never dreamed that I was just outside the window watching him, and—no, I wouldn't do that, Miss Paul," she broke off to say, while she swiftly brought her revolver into play. "Sit down. That is better.

"I intend that you shall listen to all that I have to say, so you may as well compose yourself. I know murder is an unpleasant subject of conversation, but there are certain things which must be said to you, and I intend to say them. Now then, where was I? Oh yes, at the part where the lad was in a very critical position.

"It may have occurred to you to wonder, since I witnessed what was going on, that I made no move to stop it. Let me disabuse your mind of that idea if you have it. If you will remember, the pleasant gentleman with spectacles came into the front part of the flat, in order to send the maid for a cab.

"While he was gone I slipped through the window and emptied out the poison in the bottle, and refilled it with water. And he sprayed the lad's face with that, Miss Paul, thinking all the time that it was the poison. Then I watched outside while the lad was carried out and taken away in a taxi and, Miss Paul, I followed. Now I come to a bit of news which will be a bit of a shock to you."

Then, briefly, and watching the other closely the while, Yvonne told of the accident at the level crossing.

A peculiar expression came into the eyes of Marion Paul, as she heard what Yvonne said, and she gulped several times as though seeking to say something. But, finally, she contented herself with silence, and Yvonne went on to relate what had occurred at Baker Street, and the fate which had overtaken the would-be murderer there.

"So you see," she wound up, "that misfortune has overtaken every member of the party but yourself.

"But I think it must be very evident to you that the truth will be out as soon as Sexton Blake reaches London, and hears what is the outcome of what he suspected. He did suspect from the very first that the death of Harold Craig was an inside job; and from what I have told you, you can see that you have been under surveillance ever since he had that suspicion.

"I came on here alone in order to tell you this, because I have seen the suffering which has been the portion of Marion Fenmore. I vowed to avenge her; but when I started to do so, the regaining of the necklace was the extent of my plans. I wanted to see you suffer as she had suffered, because all other things aside it was you and Harold Craig who ruined Bob Fenmore financially.

"It is now ten o'clock. Sexton Blake arrives in London at half-past ten, and the chances are he will come straight on here. He may stop to pick up Inspector Thomas on his way, but I think we may reckon on them arriving by eleven. Now have you anything to say? If you have, I should like to hear it. I should hate to leave you believing that you had not one word to utter in extenuation of the things to which you at least lent your countenance."

As she finished speaking Yvonne leaned back a little and regarded the other. Then she started to her feet, as without the slightest warning Marion Paul slipped to the floor in a dead faint.

Yvonne reached for a bottle of smelling-salts which stood on a table near by, and in a few minutes had succeeded in bringing the prostrate woman round.

When she looked up and saw Yvonne bending over her, she rested her head against the chair in which she had been sitting and broke into a torrent of weeping. Yvonne put the smelling-salts to one side, and, bending down, tried to soothe her, but for some time the other would not be comforted.

Then gradually her sobs grew less agonised, and when Yvonne drew her head into her lap Marion Paul let it remain there. Then while

Yvonne's soft fingers stroked her head she started to speak.

At first the words came slowly and haltingly, but after a few moments her voice gathered strength, and soon she was pouring out a tale which was one of the most startling Yvonne had ever heard.

"Oh, I am glad—glad he is dead!" She said tensely. "For the last seven years I have lived in torture. When I met him in Vienna I fell into his toils, and he forced me to marry him. From that moment I have known no peace. He was a fiend incarnate. We had to flee from Vienna because he forced me to act as decoy to a man there, so that he would swindle him of all his money, as he forced me to play into Harold Craig's hands in ruining Bob Fenmore."

"Of whom do you speak?" asked Yvonne gently.

"Of the man you saw last night. He was my husband. In Vienna, when he had finished with the man there, he killed him; but so fiendishly clever was he that he was never suspected. He always arranged that if suspicion were aroused it would be I who would suffer. In Berlin he forced me to do as in Vienna. And in Paris the same. Oh, it was the same every place we went!

"And when I came to London he followed me here and forced me to do his bidding again. I did not want to injure Bob Fenmore. It was my husband who met Craig, and together they arranged his ruin. My husband wanted the money, and Craig had never forgiven him for marrying the woman he loved. I was the catspaw. I was forced to write to Fenmore, and to pretend that I cared for him. I liked him and respected him, but that was all; and I wouldn't have made Marion Fenmore suffer a single moment unless I had been forced into it.

"Always I had my husband at me egging me on to do these things, and threatening me with ruin if I refused. I told him I would have nothing to do with the ruining of Bob Fenmore, but he said if I didn't he would send an anonymous letter to the police telling them I was responsible for the death of the man in Vienna.

"If Bob Fenmore is alive, he can tell you that I did as little as possible, and more than once begged him to stop gambling. Even my maid was a spy in the service of my husband.

"Every move I made was reported to him, and I had to pretend that I was unaware of it. Oh, I prayed so that he would be caught and interned in an alien camp when war broke out. But even when I suggested this as a possibility, he said if it happened he would know that it was I who had informed on him, and that I should suffer dearly for it. I scarcely knew which way to turn.

"He had me in his grip, and only I know how awful that grip was. Then when Craig came with the letter and the necklace, I knew that neither of them was intended for me. The relations which existed between Bob Fenmore and me were never such as to inspire a letter such as that. I knew it was intended for his wife, and wanted to send it to her, but did not dare.

"Then when Fenmore had been ruined and was compelled to flee, Craig began to make himself offensive to me, and because my husband conceived the idea of ruining him next, and bleeding him of his money, he forced me to appear as though I liked his attentions. I hated Craig. Soon he began to suggest that I give him back the necklace and the letter, and I saw that was the reason he had been so attentive to me. In an unguarded moment I mentioned this to my husband, and from that moment Craig was doomed. He was bled for more money, and then my husband planned his death.

"Some time before Max, the man who met his fate at Baker Street, had gone as Craig's valet. He was another creature of my husband's, and through him my husband knew every move Craig made. That the plan to kill him was a success you have seen, though the only share I had in it was to act a part when I arrived home that night. My husband and Max arranged everything, and when my maid and I got home from the theatre it was she who destroyed the flowers."

"Then it was the flowers as Mr. Blake thought," murmured Yvonne.

The other nodded.

"Yes. The poison with which my husband sprayed them was a rare one, and he had used it many times with success. But I care not what comes now. For seven years my life has been a fraud and a torture.

"While I was in his power I was utterly helpless to do anything but submit; but now he is dead, and I am glad— glad. I am free at last, and can live my life differently. Let them arrest me—let them put me in prison—I care not. One day I shall be free again, and can make up for the misery of the past, though Heaven knows I am innocent in my heart of any wrong-doing. But I should like you to tell Marion Fenmore that I did not intentionally bring pain upon her. I should like to know that she forgave me."

"I don't think you need worry on that score," replied Yvonne softly. "But you must let me think for a moment. I needn't tell you that this has come as a great shock to me. I never dreamed that the facts were as they are, and if you are innocent and have suffered, no good could be gained by sending you to prison. The others—those who were responsible for it all—have met a fate they deserved, and it seems almost as though that same fate had saved you with a purpose. The great point is to arrange that the law shall rest satisfied with the price which has already been paid. To ensure that we must be able to prove beyond all doubt, that you are innocent, and the other three were the guilty parties."

"Oh! You believe me, don't you?" cried Marion Paul wildly.

Yvonne took her hand and pressed it.

"Of course I believe you," she answered. "The thing we must do is to make the law believe you, and I am going to help you to do that."

"You are good—good!" sobbed the other.

"There—there," said Yvonne soothingly, "you must not give way again. We have very little time in which to plan before they will be here."

As she said that, the woman who crouched at her feet caught fiercely at her skirt.

"They will arrest me, and, for what I am not guilty, I shall suffer the shame and ignominy of a trial and conviction. Oh, that would be too much! I can't bear any more."

"Hush!" ordered Yvonne sternly, seeing that the other was on the brink of another attack of hysterical weeping.

"Let me plan. I promise you I will save you if it is possible. Think carefully. Have you anything at all which will help us? Have you any letters or papers of any kind?"

Like a flash Marion Paid was on her feet.

"I have—I have!" she cried excitedly. "I have papers which my husband gave me only last night to keep for him. I have letters from him in which he threatens me if I fail to do as he bids me. I have letters of Craig's, too, which will prove that it was he who planned the ruination of Bob Fenmore, and my husband's papers will also show that Max and my maid were in the thing with him."

"Ah! Those are just what we need," responded Yvonne.

"With those I can take the necessary steps to help you. First I must win over Mr. Blake to our side, and then leave it to him to impress the police with the fact that the guilty ones have already been punished."

"Yes—yes, that is what you must do!" cried Marion Paul excitedly. "But they will soon be here, and they will not listen perhaps until it is too late."

"They will not have any other choice," replied Yvonne calmly, "because, when they arrive they will not find you here. It is half-past ten now. How long will it take you to get ready to leave? You needn't take any clothes with you. I can arrange that for you."

"I can be ready in five minutes; but where am I to go?"

"You get your things on as quickly as possible!" ordered Yvonne. "By the time you are ready, I shall have things planned out."

Without another word Marion Paul hurried from the room, and Yvonne, seating herself at the desk, wrote a brief note to Anna, her maid, who was at Queen Anne's Gate. In it she told her to receive the bearer, and to give her the guest-room, adding that she was to supply her with anything she needed. Then she cautioned Anna to observe strict secrecy about the other's presence in the house, and wound up by saying that as soon as possible she herself would come to Queen Anne's Gate and arrange matters further. By the time she had finished, Marion Paul was back in the room, and Yvonne turned to her with a smile.

"Now, then," she said, "you are to take this note to the address which is on the envelope. It is to my maid, and she will look after you until I come. You will go at once, and I should advise you to take a moving taxi rather than one off the rank. It is just as well to be careful. I shall be home some time this afternoon, and tell you how I get on with Mr. Blake. Now, run along. You mustn't be here when they come."

Marion Paul took the note, then, turning to Yvonne, she threw her arms about her, and kissed her with gratitude.

"Oh, you will never regret doing this for me!" she sobbed. "You are so good."

Then she hurried out, and Yvonne, whose eyes were suspiciously wet, lit a cigarette and ensconced herself in a big easy-chair to await the arrival of Blake. Marion Paul had been gone less than a quarter of an hour when the bell rang, and rising, Yvonne went to answer it.

As she expected, it was Blake and Tinker, and with them was Inspector Thomas. She stood aside for them to enter, and while shaking hands with Blake winked brazenly at Tinker, who stood just behind his master.

That astute young man knew something must have happened since he had parted from her, but he couldn't guess what, and contented himself with winking back as much as to say, "I can't catch your meaning, but if you want me to be mum about anything in front of the inspector, I'm as dumb as an oyster."

Yvonne nodded almost imperceptibly, then turned and led the way to the study. When they were all seated Blake opened the conversation.

"I called for Inspector Thomas and brought him along after hearing what had occurred last night," he said. "From what Tinker tells me, it seems that my first suspicions were correct. On the way here I opened two cablegrams which Tinker brought to the station with him, and before we go any further I shall tell you about them.

"Yesterday I wired to an agent in New York and one in Madrid. They had both had an extensive experience of Vienna and Berlin, and I asked them to let me have all the information they possessed regarding Marion Paul. In one of them—that which came from New York—I am told, as I thought, that she was married in Vienna to a man known as Johann Mulberg, a chemist of sorts.

"It seems that he has an exceptionally bad record in Vienna, and in the cable received from New York I am told that he is suspected of being the real cause of a certain death in Vienna, which was connected with his wife's name when she was appearing on the stage there. My agent in New York also tells me that Mulberg has made a practice of using his wife as a lure to attract his victims to his net, but how large a part she had in the business he is not prepared to say. He also adds that the impression is Mulberg was in London when war broke out, and from what I can gather of his description, together with the fact Tinker heard him called by the name of Johann here last night, which is Mulberg's first name, it seems that it was he who was killed in the taxi. If so, he has met a well-deserved fate.

"But I think it's as well that we have in Marion Paul and see what she can tell us. The inspector has brought a warrant with him, and desires to exercise it."

Yvonne gazed steadily at Blake for a moment, trying to tell him that she had information to give him but which she could not reveal to the inspector. Then she said:

"I am sorry, but Marion Paul is not here. She has left the flat, but has taken nothing with her. Perhaps she will return, and it might be a good idea for the inspector to leave a man here to await her return."

The inspector frowned with disappointment. He had hoped for the chance of serving the warrant then and there. Since Blake's entry into the case it had seemed to have drifted from his hands entirely, and the events of the previous night had upset him.

That things of such an important nature should transpire when he was not there did not suit him, but could he have arrested such a well-known figure as Marion Paul, he would have made up for much that he had missed.

He turned to Blake to see what he thought of it, but that gentleman had suddenly been stricken dumb as had Tinker a few minutes before. He had read the message in Yvonne's eyes, and, knowing she would not block matters as she was doing without sufficient reason, was quite willing to play into her hand.

So, instead of offering anything in the way of a suggestion which would give the inspector an idea what to do, he said:

"Ah, so she is not here! Then in that event I think Mademoiselle Yvonne's suggestion is the wisest course to pursue, inspector. As for me, I must return to Baker Street at once and prepare to report at Whitehall."

He rose then, and with a glint of amusement in his eyes, took leave of the inspector, who was obviously in a state great indecision. Then, as though it were an afterthought he turned to Yvonne and said:

"By the way, Yvonne, can I drop you off on the way?"

She nodded and smiled at him. Then, gathering up a thick bundle of papers which Marion Paul had placed in her hand before she left, and which the inspector never dreamed contained the material which Yvonne hoped would defeat his plans regarding the actress, she followed Blake towards the door. And so they departed, leaving the inspector in command of the field. When they were once in a taxi and speeding towards Baker Street, Blake turned to her and said:

"Now, then, young lady, explain why you have taken it upon yourself to defeat the ends of justice?"

She glanced at him demurely.

"Wait until we get to Baker Street, and I will tell you everything," she said.

And with that he had to rest content. But when they were in the consulting-room Yvonne seated herself and related all that had happened since she left Tinker earlier in the morning, even telling him where she had sent Marion Paul for safety. Blake nodded thoughtfully when she had finished.

"I guessed that might be the case," he said slowly. "And if it is, then it would be a great injustice if she were punished. It would not gain anything for justice and would but ruin her life uselessly. I think you can safely leave it to me, Yvonne, to handle the inspector on this matter, and after the inquest on the victims of the accident as well as on the unfortunate creature who met his death here when he was planning mine, I think the police will consider the matter closed."

"Then you don't blame me for the step I took?" she asked.

"Certainly not. You did quite right. It was only a sample of what you are always ready to do for others. Which, by the way, brings me to the point where I want to tell you how grateful both Tinker and myself are for what you did for him last night. It is plain that you saved his life with imminent risk to yourself, and though neither of us are very good hands at expressing our gratitude, we appreciate it very deeply."

Yvonne flushed warmly, and tried to stammer some inconsequential reply, when Blake continued:

"And now I would suggest that we all adjourn to the Venetia for an early lunch. I have some great news for you."

"Oh, is it about Bob Fenmore?" cried Yvonne eagerly.

"You guessed right the first time," laughed Blake. "Come along and I shall tell you."

A WEEK later Sexton Blake made another journey to France, but this time it was not on a mission for the British Government. The preceding seven days had been very busy ones, and this journey was the last duty he had to do before bringing to a finish that which he had promised Yvonne to accomplish, if possible.

In addition to other cases which had come up, he had had several interviews with Inspector Thomas regarding what action should or should not be taken against Marion Paul. Partly owing to the undoubted evidence at the inquest, backed up by the papers which Yvonne had received from Marion Paul, and partly because he knew Blake would not make such a request unless he knew his ground well, the inspector finally decided to call the matter closed, and, through Yvonne, Blake sent the good news to Marion Paul, Then, when he could get away, he had started for France. While he was absent Tinker and Yvonne had much to do, they had planned a surprise, over which they were as gleeful as children—at least, Yvonne, Tinker, and Pedro were, while Blake smiled tolerantly.

He did not blind himself to the fact that he had a difficult proposition ahead of him; but when, the next day, he was shown into a room at the — Hospital, where a certain Private Fraser lay convalescing, he showed only confidence in his bearing.

At a sign from him the nurse left him alone with the patient, and as soon as the door had closed after her Blake walked over to the bed.

"Well, Fenmore," he said cheerfully, "aren't you about tired of this game?"

The man in the bed half rose, then sank back. Only his eyes showed the sudden blaze of memory caused by the use of the old name.

"Who—who are you?" he asked.

"They call me Sexton Blake," replied Blake quietly. "And now listen, Fenmore. I wish to speak to you as man to man, and when I finish I am going to make arrangements for you to accompany me back to England."

Then Blake began, and talked in a low tone of many things which no man might know but he who uttered them and he who listened. They were things of an intimate nature, but though they might not be revealed to the world, it may be said that when Blake had finished

150

Bob Fenmore's head was sunk on his arm, and he was weeping unashamed.

Then Blake rose softly, and, without a backward look, went out to make arrangements for departure. That night a motor left the — Hospital for Calais, and in the tonneau sat Sexton Blake, with the huddled-up figure of a wounded British soldier beside him.

They reached Calais shortly after midnight, and went to the hotel, to remain until morning. There Bob Fenmore was met by a Red Cross nurse whom he did not remember because he had been delirious when carried into the hospital, but whom Blake had told him had nursed him during the first part of his illness.

It was the Hon. Edwina Stafford, who, at Blake's request, had come to Calais to meet the wounded man and to look after him on the way back. Blake had told her a good deal of the story, and her tender heart had gone out to Fenmore in his misery.

Then the next morning there was another surprise, for, just as they were preparing to depart, word was brought that Captain Vaughan was waiting for them with the Fleur-de-Lys at the Calais Pier.

So in Yvonne's comfortable yacht they made the passage to Dover, and finally reached London about noon. It was Christmas Eve, and London, though bowed down with care and sorrow, had responded nobly to the season. The streets were crowded as in former years, and as Fenmore gazed upon the scene his thoughts went back to that day in the trenches when all the other members of his company had received letters from home but himself. Then he turned to Blake, and, without any explanation, said:

"Thank you!"

But Blake understood. They drove at once to Baker Street, where Fenmore was to remain until it was time to carry out the rest of the programme they had arranged. Miss Stafford remained with him, and later in the day Blake, who had gone out on some mysterious business, returned with Yvonne and Tinker.

Then, about five o'clock in the afternoon, when Christmas Eve was indeed upon them, they called two taxis, and, piling in, drove to Knightsbridge.

Now, Fenmore had not been told that his wife had moved, and therefore he was much puzzled when he saw their destination. But he was in Blake's hands, and got out without protest, though inwardly he was in a fever of excitement to discover what the night was to bring him.

If it would win him the forgiveness of his wife, it was more than he dared hope for. But little did he dream of the things which were going to be revealed to him that night.

When they reached the flat he was taken along to the dining-room, which was decorated with holly, and where the table had been laid. He was surprised to see Marion Paul there; but Blake had told him enough about that for him to understand that she, too, had suffered, and when she came to him, asking if he forgave, he thought of the forgiveness he hoped for himself, and whispered:

"Yes."

Then, while the others watched with misty eyes, Blake took him by the arm, and said, "Come, Fenmore!"

He allowed himself to be led away without protest, and when Blake paused before a door and knocked, he stood quite quiescent. A muffled voice inside called "Enter!" And then Blake, turning the handle, pushed Fenmore inside.

The door closed after him, and he found himself alone. Alone? No, not alone, for there was a small figure lying on a couch which had been placed in the shadow. And then from the depths of the cushions came a soft, inviting voice:

"Well, Bob, haven't you anything to say to your wife?"

Fenmore took a step forward, then another and another; but suddenly, as his bandaged arm and shoulder were revealed beneath the light, there was a sudden eruption in the region of the couch, and Marion Fenmore came flying towards him.

"Oh, my dear—my dear!" she said. "I can't bear to see you thus!"

The next moment she was wrapped about by his sound arm, and he was whispering over her bent head:

"Can you really forgive me, Marion?"

Her soft fingers went towards his lips.

"There, dear," she said gently, "if there is anything to forgive, I have already forgiven you! I have ached for you and yearned for you so, dear!"

"And I for you, sweetheart!" he replied huskily.

"Now that I have you back I shall never risk losing you again."

"I was a mad fool, Marion, but I have paid the price."

"We have both suffered, dear one," she whispered, "but we will do differently in the future. Now come with me. I am all eagerness to show you your Christmas present."

Wonderingly, Fenmore allowed her to lead him across the room to an alcove, which was concealed by heavy portieres. Taking them, she pulled them aside, and, with a happy little laugh, thrust him in. Fenmore went ahead; then suddenly he paused, his eyes wide with unbelief. A moment he stood thus, then he stumbled forward, and fell on his knees beside a small white cradle, in which a pink[1] little baby slept. He stared at it in utter disbelief, then he turned, and from his very soul the cry went out:

"Marion! Is it—"

She was beside him ere he had finished, hiding her head against his shoulder, and blushing divinely.

"Yes, sweetheart," she whispered; "and—and we have called him Bob. But don't wake him."

Then Bob Fenmore turned, with heaving shoulders, and wrapped her close unto his heart. And so, kneeling beside that tiny white cot, did Bob and Marion Fenmore find the white road of trust and happiness which heaven reminds us of each Christmas Day.

• • • • •

That evening there was such joy in the Fenmore flat as it had never witnessed. There was feasting and toasting and many cheery tales until the clock struck midnight. Then did all hands rise and join in singing a carol of thanksgiving as the natal day was ushered in. And not one among them but looked towards Bob and Marion Fenmore with hearts that were glad.

And then they departed, leaving husband and wife together, while all the way home Blake and Yvonne carried with them the memory of the look in two pairs of eyes which they had left behind. And if Yvonne's eyes were misty when she said good-night at Queen Anne's Gate, she did not reveal the fact to Blake, while he drove home with Tinker and Pedro, and a strangely lonely feeling in his heart.

THE END.
[62300 WORDS]

---

[1] In these days baby boys were dressed in pink!   /drf

WITH THE LONDON SCOTTISH AT THE FRONT.

(Our Art'st depicts one of the many acts of bravery performed by the London Scottish in their baptism of fire.)

U. J.—No. 584.

THE FALL OF ANTWERP.

By R. THOMPSON.

By R. Thomson

"HALLO, Bob, old man, how do you feel?"

Dick Harding approached the bedside of his sick chum and, taking his hand in his, gripped it heartily. A joyful smile spread across his face as he noticed how much better Bob Denton looked.

"Yes," answered Bob, "I'm getting on fine now. But it's been pretty rotten not being able to speak to anybody for more than two minutes at a time. Rather funny that I should have been taken ill the day before I was going to enlist. Say, old man," he added enthusiastically, "how's the war going? Anything big happened?"

Dick pulled a chair up to the bed, and made himself comfortable.

"Let me see, how long have you been laid up? Nearly two months, isn't it?"

"That's right," agreed Bob.

"Well, you haven't heard about the fall of Antwerp?"

Bob started up in bed in surprise, and dropped back as Dick laid a restraining hand upon him.

"Antwerp! Fallen!" he ejaculated. "No, I haven't. But now you're here, you've got to tell me all about it. The doc. says I'm out of danger now, so it doesn't matter how long you stay. Fire away, and let's have a full account of it."

"Right-ho!" said Dick heartily. "I'll do my best. You remember that the Germans were practically conquering all Belgium. They had passed through Liege and Namur, had destroyed Louvain, and captured Brussels. When the latter fell the Belgian Government transferred their quarters to Antwerp, as the latter was supposed to be surrounded by impregnable forts.

"'Antwerp will never fall!' cried the most optimistic people. 'Its forts are far stronger than those of Namur and Liege.' But the Germans did not harbour the idea that they could not capture Antwerp. They were bent upon conquering all Belgium, so, in spite of the knowledge that the town would render a greater resistance than the other Belgian fortified cities, the German army began to approach Antwerp.

"The 11-inch guns which had wrecked the forts of Liege and Namur were brought forward by a German force numbering something like fifty thousand men, and commenced to bombard the

156

outer line of forts. There were hopes of the Belgians being able to prevent the city falling into the hands of the enemy, and they determined to resist the attack as far as was in their power.

"The forts of Liegele, Breendouck, Duffel, Waelhem, and Lierre were at first singled out for attack by the German gunners, and for the first few days they were able to give all they took. The enemy's shells crashed with increasing rapidity into the forts but the guns inside the rock-like defences thundered forth every minute, dealing out tremendous destruction.

"In the hope of beating back the Germans, the defenders entrenched between the forts kept up a deadly rain of artillery and rifle fire. By night there was no lapse in the severity of the conflict. Searchlights streamed forth from the forts, guiding the aim of the gunners. The men in the trenches, although firing for hours at a stretch, showed the same indomitable courage when rain began to fall. Soaked to the skin though they were, they fired away incessantly at the attackers.

"As hour succeeded hour, the German fire became deadlier and deadlier, and fast it became apparent that Antwerp was not so impregnable after all. Situated between the outer forts and the town of Antwerp there were many villages, and the inhabitants, terrorised at the terrible roar of battle, and fearful for their own safety, began to leave their homes for the town itself.

"Then the Belgians, eager to hamper the progress of the enemy, made a great sacrifice. They burnt these villages to the ground, and in their place erected entanglements that would at any rate, they thought, delay the German advance for some time should they succeed in passing the outer forts.

"For six whole days the bombardment of the forts continued, and then the unexpected happened. The Germans commenced a bombardment of the city itself. Their attacking force had increased to quite three hundred thousand men, and to the surprise of everyone they had brought up a number of still more powerful siege guns than those used at Liege and Namur.

"Altogether, it was estimated that no fewer than two hundred siege guns were engaged in the bombardment. Not only did the Germans possess 11 and 12-inch guns, but some of them were computed to fire 16-inch shells.

"Whilst these terrible weapons of warfare hurled their

messengers of death into the grand old city, a number of Zeppelins flew over the town and dropped a quantity of explosive bombs on the oil-tanks and waterworks. Immediately flames began to spread in all directions, and the buildings in the near vicinity caught fire.

"Louder and louder grew the noise of the guns, houses began to shake and crumple up, and the inhabitants, terror-stricken, commenced to leave the city. Thousands did not trouble about their homes—the homes that had taken them years of hard work to get together. They were concerned in one object only—their own safety. A few, more daring than the rest, delayed their flight a few hours in order to save some of their most treasured belongings, whilst others crammed hand-barrows with bedding, and as many other articles that they could ill afford to lose.

"Nevertheless, there was one constant stream of fleeing inhabitants. It was pitiful to see them. The roads were simply crammed with nervous, tearful people, children in arms, women and men in the prime of life, and aged folk who were almost unable to walk.

"Thousands were hungry, some even starving, whilst others were compelled to flee without a single belonging, and without a penny in their pockets. Some were better off than others; some were even rich. But they were all endeavouring to get away from the city in the shortest possible time.

"The Germans did not respect the rich, they did not respect the poor. No matter whether it was the poor man's cottage, the stockbroker's house, or the millionaire's mansion. They all suffered the same treatment.

"For two days and nights the German siege guns kept up the bombardment of the town. From a position some eight miles distant they hurled their gigantic shells weighing anything up to half a ton into the very heart of the city. No matter where they fell, each shell inflicted irreparable damage.

"Houses crumpled up as though they were made of match-wood. Many poor people afraid to leave the city, and equally afraid to remain in their rooms, sought refuge in the cellars. The consequence was a number of them were buried alive, for when a shell demolished their houses they were buried beneath tons of bricks and mortar. Had anybody been in the vicinity willing to help, they could not have rescued the buried ones, so huge was the mass above them.

"Before long the Central Railway station caught fire, and then, to crown everything, no less than fifty oil-tanks were one mass of roaring, gushing flames. They spread in all directions, hungrily devouring the buildings near by. Strong as they looked in times of peace, they were like pieces of paper to the blazing oil-tanks.

"The southern and eastern parts of the city soon resembled an immense bonfire, magnified several million times. A volcanic eruption is lurid enough, in all conscience, but the appearance of Antwerp in flames can only be likened to an inferno.

"The smoke from the flaring mass of burning buildings spread throughout the district, choking everybody and everything, and the German lyddite shells[2], when they burst, emitted suffocating fumes that made matters a thousand times worse.

"The heat was terrible, unbearable; in fact, the people who were unfortunate enough not to have escaped, and were in the burning parts of the town, were choked to death, so dense were the smoke and fumes.

"No man alive could have stopped the raging, burning mass. Had the fire brigades been able to turn out, they had no means of obtaining water, for German shells had long since accounted for the waterworks and brought them to a state of ruin. The buildings, once the proud homes of peaceful Belgian citizens, simply had to burn and burn, until there was not a stick left to fall a victim to the blazing furnace.

"Even some of the big buildings of the city did not come through the ordeal unscathed. The law courts were damaged, and the magnificent Gothic cathedral of Notre Dame, the Belgians' most valued church, was partly destroyed."

Bob Denton touched his chum on the arm.

"Were there any British troops in Antwerp during the siege?" he

---

[2] Lyddite was a form of high explosive widely used during both the Boer War and First World War, most notably during the latter by the British. Named after the area in southern England in which the substance's initial trials were performed so as to maintain secrecy, Lyddite was actually composed of molten and cast picric acid.
First tested in 1888 Lyddite was considered a relatively 'insensitive' explosive, which meant that it lent itself moderately well to armour piercing shells, given that the substance was less liable to detonate immediately upon impact but would instead be triggered by an impact fuse. In practice however Lyddite shells would detonate while in the process of tearing through armour.

asked.

"Yes," replied Dick. "Some eight thousand marines and bluejackets were drafted into the town for defensive purposes. And a grand part they played, too.

"But the Germans possessed a greater number of siege guns than we did, and force of numbers told once again, as they did in the siege of Liege. Several of the forts were eventually silenced by the German guns, whilst two or three were blown up by the defenders when it was found that further resistance could be of no use.

"The Waelhem and Wavre forts were amongst those which were destroyed by the Belgians themselves. But the commander of the latter had a great knock at the Germans before he gave in. A Zeppelin was hovering over the fort, and giving range to the German guns. The commander ordered the gunners to stop firing, and the Zeppelin, believing that the fort had been silenced, signalled for German infantry to advance.

"This they did, with the result that when the enemy were within a matter of yards of the fort, the Belgian guns and quick-firers burst forth into action, repulsing the attackers, and causing them to leave about eight thousand dead on the slopes about the forts.

"But the Germans were not deterred; they had a still greater force to bring forward. Gradually they forced their way onwards until they reached the burning, ruined city. When it was found that no advantage could be gained by holding out any longer, the Belgian army commenced to evacuate the town.

"Their whole army got away intact, leaving the Germany to enter the city practically unchallenged. All the while the Belgian forces were moving southwards, our tiny army of marines and bluejackets held the trenches, keeping back the Germans as long as possible, and then—"

"Yes," chimed in Bob, "what happened to them?"

"When their purpose had been accomplished," explained Dick, "they retreated. The majority of them got away to the south, whilst two thousand or so, finding themselves cut off by the German attack, were compelled to enter Dutch territory and lay down their arms.

"The retreat of both the Belgian and British forces was carried out thoroughly and almost without mishap, for even the armoured trains and heavy guns were all brought away. Antwerp fell into German hands, but the gallant defence of the allied forces will be remembered for centuries."

"Yes," cried Bob, "I bet the Germans suffered enough casualties in the bombardment. I shall be glad when the doc. says I'm well enough to quit this bed, so that I can enlist and have a knock at the beggars!"

"Good man!" replied Dick. "We'll join together!"

The End.

THE FAMOUS CHARGE OF THE LONDON SCOTTISH.

U. J.—No. 584.

THE BATTLE OF THE COAST.

The Kaiser's second "dash at all costs" was for Calais. Here, as in the case of the one for Paris, he reckoned without his foe. The Allied forces were able, after strenuous fighting, to hold the Prussians in check, and they were ably backed up by the "monitors", newly acquired by the British Government. These boats, being of shallow draught, approached quite near the coast, and wrought fearful damage with their big guns.

162

The Fleetway House, Farringdon Street, E.C.

A WORD FROM THE SKIPPER.

THE FLEETWAY HOUSE, FARRINGDON STREET, E.C.

CHEERY OH!

On this special page of mine, I cannot refrain from once more wishing all and every one of my readers the old, old wish of a Happy Christmas.

As I write, I cannot say definitely whether there is going to be, for instance, snow on the ground by the time that you read these lines, although I have done my best and nearly worried the Weather Clerk to death to try and find out. But I can imagine in my mind's eye the sort of Christmas that I hope nearly every reader is going to have.

There are jolly fine games in the morning, snow fighting and sleighing, making the snow man, and all the fun that there is to be gained in a snow-covered field. On the frozen pond a nice group of figures skating with all the vim and energy of youth. Further on a large lump of snow dropping (quite accidentally, of course!)

OFF THE WALL ON TO GRANDFATHER'S HEAD,

and a large-sized snowball, rolling down the hill, making Auntie scamper from its path as quickly as though it were a dozen mice! And so on!

That, reader, is the sort of Christmas I am wishing YOU.

As I said a fortnight ago, however, I know that many people are going to have a melancholy Christmas, and to those people who cannot possibly have such a jolly time, I hope that they will at least find consolation in their misfortunes this Yuletide.

Now please do not take this, my less happy readers, that I am giving you full licence to pull a long face and be as miserable as possible. I am not. The most wretched person at Christmas to have any dealings with is

THE PERSON WHO WILL NOT BE HAPPY WHEN HE CAN.

Many there will be, I know, who will have lost relations very dear to them, and a pall of gloom must hang over the household during the gay season. But these people, I am happy to think, will be in a minority; and I do want to urge all those of my readers who have sustained a blow through this cruel War which is, maybe, hard to bear, but at the same time not absolutely crushing, to try and forget their sorrows and join in the merrymaking. They will feel all the better for it. They will make other people happy.

AND THAT IS WHAT CHRISTMAS IS FOR.

Many readers will have read the yarn contained in this issue by the time that they come to these words. Many will not. To the first section—how did you like it? To the second section—I know you will like it! I can imagine the thousands of people who will read "A Soldier—and a Man" seated in cosy easy chairs, while a blazing log burns on the hearth, and the room is decorated with holly and mistletoe, simply revelling in the fine Christmassy flavour of the adventures which are chronicled.

I know that you will admit that I have done my share to make Christmas enjoyable; now I want you to do yours. You will be able to do this in quite a number of ways; not the least of them will be to pass this copy on to someone else, especially, say, one of our brave soldiers, at the front who will have to spend their Christmas

IN THE FROZEN TRENCHES OF FRANCE AND BELGIUM.

But this one copy can only be given away once—by you, at any rate. So, to do the best you can with it, you will have to use discretion. Personally, I should advise you to send your copy to a soldier abroad who has not the chance of buying one himself from a bookstall. Then, if you have a chum in England to whom you would have liked to lend your copy, just tell him something about the yarn this week, and, unless I am a very bad judge, he will at once purchase a copy himself. Then, when he has read his, he, too, can send it to someone who will appreciate it, although they may not be in a position to buy one, and in this way two copies instead of the one will be sent to someone very deserving.

JUST A WORD HERE ABOUT NEXT WEEK'S "U. J."

which will, as usual, be one penny. The title of the story is "The White Feather," and it is another fine yarn from the pen of the ever popular author of the "Carlac" and "Hon. John Lawliss" series. There is plenty of detective work in it, in addition to the strong human theme of the story, and you will all, I am sure, enjoy reading the adventure of the hero—a boy who wants, in spite of his father's objections, to enlist. When I tell you that it is well up to the usual high standard of our yarns, you will, I know, roll up for it in your thousands.

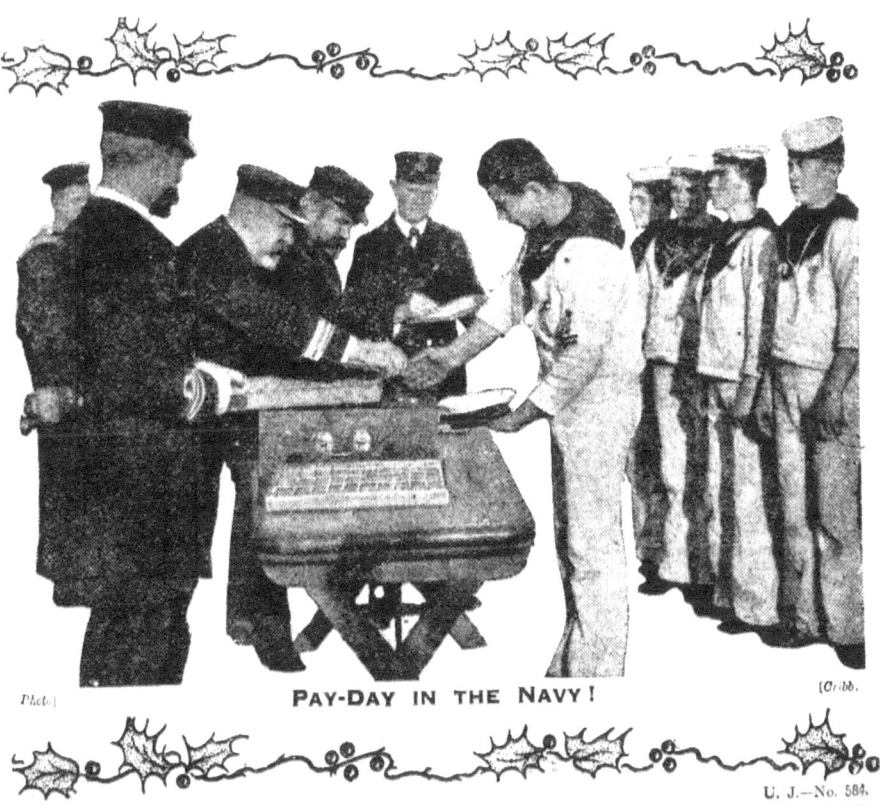

PAY-DAY IN THE NAVY!

Photo.] [Cribb.

U. J.—No. 584.

HER ROYAL HIGHNESS PRINCESS MARY APPEALS TO ALL "U. J." READERS:

"BUCKINGHAM PALACE,
"October 15th, 1914.

"For many weeks we have all been greatly concerned for the welfare of the sailors and soldiers who are so gallantly fighting our battles by sea and land. Our first consideration has been to meet their more pressing needs, and I have delayed making known a wish that has long been in my heart for fear of encroaching on other funds, the claims of which have been more urgent.

"I want you all now to help me to send a Christmas present from the whole nation to every sailor afloat and every soldier at the front. On Christmas-eve when, like the shepherds of old, they keep their watch, doubtless their thoughts will turn to home and to the loved ones left behind, and perhaps, too, they will recall the days when as children they were wont to hang out their stockings wondering what the morrow had in store.

"I am sure that we should all be the happier to feel that we had helped to send our little token of love and sympathy on Christmas morning, something that would be useful and of permanent value, and the making of which may be the means of providing employment in trades adversely affected by the war. Could there be anything more likely to hearten them in their struggle than a present received straight from home on Christmas Day?

"Please, will you help me?　　　　MARY."

To H.R.H. THE PRINCESS MARY,
BUCKINGHAM PALACE, LONDON.
I beg to enclose £　　　s.　　　d.
as a donation to your Royal Highness's Fund
Name
Address
U.J. — No. 584